BEING LUCY

The Story of a Recluse

Dale Lorna Jacobsen

On the forestry road to Mount Delusion, in the Victorian High Country, stand two old huts known as Strobridge's huts. The two-roomed hut facing the road, built of milled timber around 1935, is the more recent. This was Lucy's hut. Behind is a much older hut of slab walls and bark roof with a dirt floor—Ella's hut.

This story is based on the life of Lucy Strobridge from Brookville in the Gippsland Mountains of Victoria. Very little is known of this reclusive woman who lived her life in isolation. While I have tried to be true to the facts of her life, it is, nevertheless, a work of fiction.

Prologue

8 JANUARY 2001

The dying forest perches on the side of a mountain in silence. No birds flit through its leafless, lifeless branches, stark white against a clear blue sky. Leaves lie thick upon the ground, decaying into a rich mulch that no longer smells of peppermint. Once, these trees would have welcomed this gift; would have drawn the richness upwards to feed the tips of their limbs, but now each trunk bears a ring from an axe. The cycle is broken.

The thick mulch muffles my footfall as I weave my way through the forest, pushing a wheelbarrow, carefully avoiding new seedlings taking advantage of the light. The rubber soles of my sneakers do little to disturb the unnatural silence. I remove an axe from the barrow and lean heavily on its handle, annoyed at the need to catch my breath from the climb up the steep slopes of Dingo Ridge. Not too many years ago I had worked my way across this slope, ring barking the gums, swinging my axe without the need of rest or food.

Fatigue will not leave my old body, so I sit on a log to await another burst of energy. It will come in time. Skinks and beetles scurry through the litter at my feet, offering promise of life that will return as the seedlings grow, appeasing my conscience at having robbed the forest for my own needs.

A breeze drifts over the ridge, ruffling the hem of my cotton dress against my bare legs. I button my cardigan against its chill and rise from the log. I tap tree after tree with the back of my axe, listening to the ring it produces on the dead trunks, judging each for its readiness for falling. Young trees die more quickly than larger, older ones, and for this I am grateful, given my failing strength. I make my choice: a gun-barrel-straight trunk I can just embrace at chest height, clear of other trees that would stop its fall. I spread my feet shoulder-width apart and, getting my balance, feel the weight of the axe in my hands. The blade, honed on a stone I keep for the purpose, bites cleanly into the wood. I cut a deep wedge with a dozen strokes then move to the opposite side of the tree, checking over my shoulder that my aim is true.

The dense wood which gives such reliable heat when burnt blunts the axe and tires my muscles, but I press on, angrily jerking the blade as it jams in a fresh cut. Finally, I hear the tree creak and feel its shudder through my feet. Wisps of hair escape my woollen beanie, sticking to the beads of sweat forming on my forehead. Again, I lean on the upended axe, hand on hip, and watch the tree fall slowly, bouncing on outstretched limbs as it comes to rest on the forest floor. It makes a comfortable seat for me to catch my breath.

Measuring an axe-handle length along the trunk (the same as the length I had made my barrow) I laboriously chop the first fire log from the rest of the tree. I cradle one end of the log in my arms and tilt it onto the barrow.

I begin down the slope, struggling to hold back the load until I join the network of paths created by years of pushing the barrow across Dingo Ridge. To the untrained eye, these paths differ little from the wallaby and wombat tracks through the bush, and in truth, all the tracks are made by creatures of the mountain, for that's what I am. On the lower slopes, peppermint gums give way to manna gums and giant tree ferns line the path to my huts. This forest is safe from the bite of my axe. These trees do not burn clean and hot.

I wheel my barrow through the doorway to my cooking hut and empty my load beside the fire that smoulders day and night, year by year, blackening the walls and roof. Its pit, dug into the earthen floor, and the two flat rocks that once supported my cooking pot, are long buried beneath a pile of ash that swirls as I feed the new log to the heart of the fire. Collecting a kettle, I follow a narrow path beaten by my daily trips through the blackberries and ferns to my water source beside the hut. Lizards scurry in the undergrowth and little birds flit from tree fern to tree fern. I plunge the kettle into the water and hurry back, spilling a good measure of water on the way.

I sit on a wooden chair by the table and wait for the kettle to boil. Once, this table and chair had belonged to a handsome dining set with six chairs, each topped by a hand-carved lyrebird across its top. I could only use one chair—I don't entertain visitors—and so I used them as kindling. The one I have kept is worn to the shape of my body.

Steam puffs from the kettle's spout and I take the tea caddy from the kitchen hutch and measure two large scoops into a china teapot. I select a tea set with purple pansies from a dozen cups and saucers, each bearing a different pattern, and place it on the table as I wait for the tea to draw.

Night closes in early where I live. By three in the afternoon the sun disappears behind the highest of the mountains stretching up into alpine ash country. Day-birds give way to night-birds and a wombat shuffles from its hole in the bank beneath my cooking hut to begin its prowl up Dingo Ridge. It scratches its back on the jagged boards along the side wall, as it does every night. I am so used to the rasping noise, I barely notice; it is just another part of my day. I remove my beanie and comb my grey hair, piling it on top of my head, pinning it in place with two large bobby pins, then sip my tea.

*

With a new day, the wombat returns to its burrow. I wonder how many generations have passed beneath my floor. Despite feeling weary, I climb Dingo Ridge again to gather more firewood. I look at the tree I felled yesterday and realise I no longer have the strength to continue cutting fire-sized logs from it.

I search for something smaller that I can handle more easily and see a wattle about the right size. The crystal-clear air carries the voices of bushwalkers further along the track heading for Mount Delusion. Perhaps it is this that makes me lose concentration for a moment as I swing my axe into the trunk of the wattle. It isn't very thick; only takes a couple of blows to bring it down. I should have anticipated this, but am taken by surprise when the axe passes through and the tree falls. I begin to run from its path, but it slews sideways and lands with a crunch on my ankle, pushing me to the ground.

I lift the trunk from my leg, shocked to see the bloody pulp of the wound. I wriggle my toes—nothing broken—but, oh, the pain!

For most of my adult life I have tended to my own wounds and this time is no different. My immediate worry is to keep it clean, so I feel for my petticoat beneath my cotton skirt. It will do for a bandage. I grab the hem firmly and tear upwards towards my waist, then again, separating a strip from the garment. I wrap it around my ankle tightly, feeling nauseous with pain. It is impossible to stand from my sitting position, and so I roll onto my side. Blackness.

When I come to, I lie listening to the noises that signal the end of the day—wrens in a final feeding before roosting; goodnight laughter from a family of kookaburras—and shiver violently. I rise on my hands and knees in an attempt to stand upright, but cannot. Although winter is still some weeks off, the evening temperature plummets with the setting sun and I know that, clothed in a simple cotton dress, I need to either make my way down to my home or find shelter. I remember the little cave that has been my refuge in times of trouble and, pushing my body further up the slope with my good leg, I reach its entrance as night closes in. The soft earthen floor feels comforting as I lie on my back and try to ignore the burning from my leg.

This is Lucy's Story

1928

I pluck two freshly unfurled crosiers from a tree fern and poke them into my belt so they curl across my back. I become a lyrebird as I twirl through the flickering sunlight. I dig my bare toes deep into the damp moistness where worms and beetles burrow. Shoes are foreign to my feet, except when snow covers the mountain, then I pull on a pair of rubber gumboots. Beneath my dancing feet, the musty odour rises to mingle with the pervading smell of eucalypt. A large black beetle scurries from beneath my foot, climbing onto a twig and, spreading its wings, flies so close I can feel the beating of its wings on my cheek.

'Fly away ladybird, your house is on fire.'

I know it isn't a ladybird. That doesn't matter. I am a lyrebird, and a lyrebird can say whatever it wishes from its hiding place among the ferns. This is my forest. I know each trunk, each tree fern. I follow the paths that wind through the undergrowth, seeking the animals that have made them: wallabies with white stripes on their pretty faces; dingoes that sleep until evening rouses them. Occasionally, I find the animals and study them from behind a tree as they snooze, unaware I am watching. When I am alone, I mimic their moves and their calls until I feel I am half-animal, half-girl.

That's what lyrebirds do.

I know this mountain well, with its special trees and secret animal tracks. Once, I shadowed a dingo to the very top before it turned and held me with its yellow eyes. It stretched its neck and howled. I lifted my face and answered as the animal melted into the trees.

A twist of cloud rises from the valley floor to wind its way through the grey-green trees that cloak Mount Delusion, curling out of the far side of the ravine. I press my ear to the trunk of a tree, listening for the sap moving beneath the dark fibrous bark, feeling its roughness on my cheek. Above, two thick cream-coloured branches creak together as the air stirs again.

All day I have heard fallers working on the mountainside. Periodically, a giant crashes to earth, sending vibrations through my dancing feet. Black cockatoos screech protest in crazed circles.

I do not like the timber-getters, the way they yell to each other, using words I am forbidden to utter, and I hate the jubilation in their cheers as a tree falls. I've seen them, atop a dray pulled by draught horses, rumbling along the track past my home. Rough men.

Too soon, night comes and I head down the mountainside to my home. I push open the door made of offcut floorboards and enter to the smell of wood smoke and rabbit stew. Ma is skilfully sliding a short-bladed knife beneath the skin of a potato, streaking the exposed white flesh with dirt. A long ribbon of peel spirals off and floats on the surface, then sinks into the muddy water in the iron basin. She reaches for the next spud without raising her eyes.

'Where've you been, girl? Jehovah knows if you've been with them loggers.'

I do not share my mother's faith; to me, God does not exist, especially not to spy on me in my private life, but knowing how my tongue, thick and lazy, will distort my words into unintelligible mumbo-jumbo, I keep them inside my head.

If Jehovah knows anything about me, he would know that the last place I would be is with the loggers.

Not expecting an answer, Ma scoops a handful of potatoes from the basin and crosses to a pot bubbling on the firepit. Smoke drifts through the slab walls and bark roof, working its way past a protective patchwork of corrugated iron sheets. As the fire settles into coals, the smoke eases and the hut warms. She removes the heavy lid and slices the spuds into the thin stew, then wipes her swollen red knuckles on her apron, nodding towards the basin with wordless instruction to me. I lift the basin by its wire handles and tip the dirt-saturated water onto some mint growing by the door.

From beside the fire Billy, my brother, watches as I hang the basin from a nail on the wall. A smile spreads across his thin, pointed face as I remove a multi-coloured knitted rug from his twisted legs.

I squat, waiting, while Billy winds his arms around my neck and climbs from the cane chair onto my back. I link my hands beneath his bony bottom and hoist him higher. Ma turns from the fire.

'Where're you two going?'

'I need a pee,' says Billy.

'Don't be long then, dinner's nearly ready.'

Free of the house, we chatter in our secret language. Billy has no trouble understanding my words and we have developed our own names for the trees, the pademelons and the striped skinks that share our yard, using words I can say. Ma has long since given up trying to follow our conversations. She thinks me a strange one: refusing to speak properly, although it's as plain as the nose on her face that I understand everything that goes on. She thinks me a naughty girl too, at times, with a fierce will she can't control like a mother ought.

In the fading daylight, I sit Billy on a large rock for him to pee a golden arc onto a shrub as I tell him of the trees that have fallen that day. Billy, just seven years old (I am nine), is as appalled at the loss as I am.

'If I was a man, I'd shoot their bloody heads off.'

'If I was a man, I'd bloody join you.'

Swearing is a guilty pleasure we enjoy beyond the reach of Ma's ears.

We are galloping around the house, with Billy jiggling and giggling on my back, when Dad appears around the corner of the hut, weary from his day at the sawmill.

'You two up to no good?' he says, packing tobacco into the bowl of his clay pipe. He takes Billy and the three of us go in to eat our meal of rabbit stew.

*

Waking before first light, I lie on my stretcher absorbing the complete silence from outside. Branches that normally rustle a greeting to the early-morning breeze hang cloaked in snow that peaks along their lengths like the spines of a water dragon. Even the birds are silent.

I tip-toe to the window, pulling a blanket around my thin cotton nightie, to view the white mounds hiding yesterday's tree ferns. The sky lightens and the mounds glisten beyond the clearing. Billy stirs on his stretcher, but doesn't waken. I turn back to the white world beyond the splintery window frame, vaguely aware of the guttural snoring from Dad and the slow, deep breathing of Ma. I smile with the pleasure of having this magic to myself, at least for now.

I collect the kettle and softly close the door behind me, dragging the hem of Dad's grey woollen greatcoat across the ground as I walk in the bracing air. I step, heel then toe, through the new snow that crunches beneath my gumboots, and my cheeks tingle.

The coming of the snow marks the end of timber felling until next spring. Tomorrow, the men will load their tents and axes onto a dray and draught horses will weave their way down the steep track and peace will once again return to my mountain.

Leaving the kettle on a rock, I climb a small rise behind the hut and kick the loose snow from three wide boards. I lift the central board and squat over the hole. The chill air nips at my bare bottom, but it will get a lot worse before winter finishes.

I clamber back down the hill and grub around beneath low shrubs, feeling for warm eggs laid by the half dozen chooks that wander around the yard. In a couple of weeks, as each day grows shorter, there will be no more eggs and Ma will stew their sinewy flesh until it softens, then later boil their bones with potatoes, meal upon meal, until no trace of chook flavour remains.

With the eggs safely stowed in my coat pocket, I scramble through the rushes and ferns lining the bank to fill the kettle. In the kitchen, I stoke the fire and balance the cast-iron kettle on the flat rocks either side of the flames. Ma emerges from behind the hessian wall that separates our parents' bedroom from Billy's and mine, pinning up her plait ready to prepare eggs and hot tea.

'Got the kettle on, Lucy?'

Every morning, the same question, even though she can feel the heat from the fire already warming the room. It is her way of bidding good morning to me. I wake Billy and piggy-back him out to his rock and his bush.

After breakfast, I grow glum as I collect my slate and chalk for school. I can't see the need for attending lessons two days a week—each day reciting times tables that I can easily remember the first time I hear them. I can read much better than Ma and Dad, but find no use for the words I am compelled to learn. It would be different if the teacher taught us useful things like how to set a rabbit trap, or hone an axe on a slab of rock until the razor-sharp edge shines like a polished gem Dad could use to shave off his beard.

Billy climbs onto my back and I carry him to the one-roomed schoolhouse on the Carroll's farm where the teacher attempts to impart his wisdom to nine children from the district.

1930

The year brings worry to the Strobridge household. Lucy's father is taken ill—they say he has diabetes—and Ella is beside herself with worry, wondering what sin she has committed for Jehovah to take such revenge upon her family. She discusses this with the Brothers who visit from Bairnsdale, but they don't show any sympathy, saying: 'This is to be expected when a Witness marries a worldly person. It is Jehovah's way of letting you know that you have failed. It is a test. Bring your family into the Fellowship, and you will be spared. If you don't, you will be killed at Armageddon along with all non-Witnesses. Jehovah has no time for those who do not follow the Watchtower's teachings'.

Ella reads her Bible longer and prays more fervently convinced that, in the days of The New System after Armageddon, there will be no more illness for the faithful, but she can't convince any of her family to follow her lead and it breaks her heart.

*

I mount my horse, Ginger, and pull Billy up onto the saddle behind me. He wraps his arms around my waist. Somewhere above, the sun shines, but its rays do not reach the floor of the wet forest and won't until the middle of the day in the middle of next summer, and then only for a couple of weeks.

As we ride past tree ferns and low shrubs between tall manna gums the only sound, apart from the pad of Ginger's hooves, is the gurgle of the creek where lyrebirds hide among the sword ferns. A mile further up the hill, the forest changes. Manna gums give way to peppermint gums and these trees, with their narrow leaves, allow more sunlight to penetrate.

Years before, when our family had moved into the deserted gold miner's hut on the corner of Charlotte Spur Track, I had gone out with Dad to collect branches fallen from the manna gums, only to find that the wood remained wet and would not burn, unlike the peppermint gum growing further up the ridge, which gave a clean, hot flame. And so Dad and I ringbarked a stand of the narrow-leafed gum. When the trees eventually died, we returned with the axe to chop them into fire-length logs.

The track grows steeper as we leave the ridge, winding up the side of Mount Delusion to the west where, once again, the forest changes. Messmate, with large leaves and rough, stringy bark that extends to the very tips of the branches, tower above dense undergrowth that makes the going heavy. We continue up the mountain as pademelons hop from our path and birds dart before us.

When I was a small girl, I used to chase the dogs around the farmhouse and chatter to my parents and my big sister, Maude, about the cows and horses—never realising that the words that formed perfectly in my head made no sense to anyone else. Only when Ma had said, 'For God's sake Lucy, can't you talk like a normal person?' did I hear how my words sounded to everyone else. From that moment, I've found it easier to point to things I want and nod or shake my head in response to questions. Although I practise forming words while I lie in the gullies, waiting for the lyrebird to begin its chorus, my tongue won't respond as it should.

I'm rarely without Billy by my side and he is quick to speak for me. He reads my mind more than my lips and together we have worked out ways of communicating that no-one else can fathom. When, at the age of five, Billy contracted poliomyelitis and his legs twisted, the bond between us deepened with the understanding that we each now bore a handicap that made us different from everyone else.

Maude and I share a very different relationship. Five years older than me, she is always moving onto the next phase of life just as I think I am catching up. By the time I was looking forward to going to school, Maude was already dreaming of what life would be like when she was free to leave the farm. Each morning, as we milk the cows then walk the cans to the Brookville dairy, I see the look in Maude's eye as she imagines continuing ten miles along the road to Swifts Creek village. This week, she finally got her wish and left to work as a domestic at the Albion Hotel. I don't miss her, but it was easier when we shared the load of the milk can.

I stop when we reach the top of the mountain—more a plateau than a peak—to look out over ridges spreading in all directions. I dismount and Billy slides onto my back. We sit on a log beneath a gnarled old snow gum to eat our lunch.

'Can we go to Grandma's farm?' asks Billy.

I shake my head, and Billy knows we are not supposed to go there on our own.

'No-one'll know if we don't tell them,' he pleads.

It is autumn, and the risk of being caught in a storm is ever-present, especially if we are out late, but I want to visit the farm as much as Billy does. We have heard so much about it from Grandma since she moved to Brookville seven years ago to live with Uncle Jeff. I sniff the breeze and decide there's very little danger of a storm today.

We quickly finish our sandwiches and, back on Ginger, fly through the trees along a spur on the southern side of Mount Delusion heading for the farm by Wentworth River.

I lean into the stirrups, lifting my body, lying almost flat along Ginger's body. Each year there seems to be more deadwood lying on the ground. For as long as I can remember, the cattlemen have set fire to the grass as they leave the mountains each autumn, ensuring fresh feed the following spring. In days past I could gallop freely but now I need to keep my wits about me as Ginger leaps over logs and dodges saplings. Billy clings to my waist, whooping with joy.

Wentworth River is only inches deep where we cross the rocky ford. On the other side, we ride through scrub wattle and ti-tree until we come to an overgrown track leading away from the river through a dense forest of wattle, peppermint gum and the occasional woolly butt.

In the centre of the forest is a large clearing surrounded by trees ringbarked years ago. On a grassy hill on the edge, two huge tree trunks lie along the ground. A roof of bark fills the gap between the two logs that had once been Grandma's house. A chimney of stone is in the end wall nearest us. The logs have begun rotting into the ground. Dilapidated sheds and stables of rough-sawn boards are all around.

Behind a fallen-down fence, rabbit holes almost obliterate the remnants of Grandma's vegie garden. An apple tree twists from a tangle of gooseberries and blackberries. I have no memory of Grandpa who brought his family to live here in 1910—a tough man, according to Dad, who expected the same from his sons as they ringbarked and cleared the land, built fences, then spent weeks chopping two huge alpine ash trees and hauling them into place using just ropes and two strong horses. It formed the basis of this home for Grandma, Grandpa and their six kids.

Dad and his brothers, Jeff and George, often talk about the pigs they reared—of how the old man and 'His boys' took the pigs to the Bairnsdale markets, dropping cobs of maize from the back of the dray to encourage the pigs to follow, and slept beside the track when the pigs wanted to sleep. When they think I am not listening, they speak of his tough ways as a father and of his auburn whiskers he trimmed, when needed, with kerosene and a candle flame, but of his mysterious disappearance six months after my birth, they simply mutter: 'There's lots of mine shafts up in them mountains; he must've fallen down one of them'.

From his perch on my back, Billy pushes open the door. Seven years of mould and dust stir inside. I step into the dim room and set Billy down onto the powdery dirt floor that had once shone hard and smooth beneath Grandma's ti-tree broom. As our eyes grow accustomed to the dimness we see curtains of drooping hessian dividing the space into four rooms and one, which had been

Grandma and Grandpa's room, still has an old bed. The only light comes from a small window on the far wall. It is caked with mould and dirt.

I gather wood and kindling and return to light a fire in the huge fireplace. Having come this far, we want to sit awhile and imagine life in this unusual home. Billy tells ghost stories; I tell murder stories. We feed the fire and our imagination, laughing, singing songs. Then comes a knock on the door.

'Anyone in there?' It is a gruff voice. We sit in hushed silence, waiting for its owner to go away. The door creaks open and the silhouette of a man holding his hat in his hands fills the frame. He turns to speak to someone waiting beyond the door, 'It's only a couple of kids'. Another silhouette joins the first. I rise from the fire, holding Billy's hand tightly.

'Mind if we join you?' the man asks.

I stand motionless, staring at the two strangers.

'This is our house!' shouts Billy.

'Your house, eh? I understood it was deserted. Look young fella, we don't mean you no harm, we just want somewhere to bunk down for the night, we'll be off at first light.'

'It's our grandma's house! Nobody's allowed here but us!'

'Doesn't look much like a house to me, more like a barn.'

'Or a tree house,' laughs his companion. They both laugh at that.

I hoist Billy onto my back and one of the men makes a neighing noise and slaps his thigh with his hat. 'Giddy-up.'

We run from the house to the ringing of laughter.

*

Ma watches us during the evening meal. I know we are unusually quiet, even for me.

'What have you two been up to?'

'Nothing,' replies Billy.

'I know you like I know the back of me hand; you been up to something.'

Billy looks at me and reads my voiceless instruction to stay silent as I deliver a gentle kick to his shins. I bend my head to my meal, but can't dismiss the thought that strangers are sleeping in Grandma's house.

The next morning is Sunday, the day for Jehovah God, and as the nearest Kingdom Hall is a full day's ride away at Bairnsdale, Ma makes up for it by washing and dressing in her best frock in order to spend the Holy Day reading her Bible and praying—activities which she expects us, her family, to join in. We mostly do, as it is easier than hearing Ma's predictions of eternal damnation. Billy waits until Ma has torn a sheet of newspaper into squares and disappears towards the toilet hole before approaching Dad to tell of the previous day's visit. Billy isn't afraid of a cuff around the ears. It has been a long time since he or I have felt the back of Dad's hand: Billy because he is so frail he could not withstand the force; me because I have grown so fast it will not be long until I am as tall as Dad.

'Dad, we went to Grandma's farm yesterday, and two blokes came in. They said they were going to sleep there.'

Dad doesn't look up from packing his pipe. 'No harm done, so long as they don't set fire to it.'

'But Dad, they laughed at us. And Grandma's house. Called it a tree house.'

Dad's hands pause momentarily, then continue working the tobacco into the bowl.

'They called Lucy a horse because she piggy-backed me.'

Dad stands, tucks his tobacco pouch into his waistcoat pocket, clenching his pipe between his teeth, and is collecting his hat from the peg by the door when Ma returns. She is taken aback at the sight of Dad preparing to leave the house.

'Where do you think you're going?'

'I've got things to do. I'm off to see Jeff.'

He puts his hat on his head, muttering, as he closes the door with more force than it deserves: 'Think they can laugh at us Strobridges. We'll show them who has the last laugh'.

Ma repositions a hairpin in her plait and smooths a few loose strands. She bows her head and Billy and I obediently do likewise as we listen to the beat of hooves fade along Charlotte Spur Track.

*

The two brothers watch from a thicket of wattle, checking for signs of other humans—hobbled horses, smoke from the chimney, saddle bags hanging from a branch—but there are none. They dismount, dropping the reins to the ground. Johnny and Jeff cross the open ground to the rise, gathering dried branches for fuel as they go.

The old place is a reminder of extreme poverty in isolation and a father with whiskers and hair as red as fire who whipped pigs and sons alike—until he disappeared. People had laughed at the family and its strange house.

No more.

Jeff and Johnny both light matches and toss them to the pile of dried leaves and grass they heap on the dirt floor.

1932

Hunger forces rabbits from their burrows in search of green shoots that grow ever more elusive with the deepening snow drifts. Each day they forage further into the forest, nibbling the tips of fern fronds that are too fine to hold the weight of snow.

In deep ravines, where the land folds in on itself and the sun never reaches, moss and lichen take hold on rocks of all sizes capped by fresh snow. To reach this rich harvest, the rabbits follow a path that winds along the floor of the ravine like a white creek. But grey fur on white makes an easy target, easy pickings for the wedge-tailed eagle perched high, watching. The eagle sweeps along the valley floor, so narrow that its black and tan wings almost touch the sides. Beads of bright blood track along the white snow as talons dig deep into the rabbit flesh.

Ella takes a handkerchief from her apron pocket and wipes clear a circle on the window pane misted by her breath. She shudders at the cold outside, despite the warmth within the hut—or perhaps it is the sight of Billy bouncing about on that wretched trolley. His bony little bottom will be red raw by the time he and Lucy return, but all Ella's reasoning cannot prevent him from going with Lucy. In truth, he derives very little pleasure from living the life of a cripple. He will never walk again, the doctor says—very few polio victims ever do—and so she bites her tongue and adds an extra layer of flannel over his delicate chest. She watches until the dimness of the forest swallows the children, then returns to her chores.

*

I lower Billy onto the splintery deck of the trolley and tuck his rug around and beneath his legs. The trolley and the rug are both of my making, but I do not feel pride in their appearance, I keep my pride for the pictures I draw when I am alone. Making items for use is just something I do—like setting a line of rabbit traps.

I pile a dozen traps around Billy and sling another couple from my shoulders, then step into the loop of rope fastened to the front of the trolley. I wrap the rope around my waist and lean into it, head forward, my body almost bent double until the old pram wheels slowly turn, parting the snow, to leave two ruts in their wake.

The path we take skirts the steep, heavily timbered slopes. Fresh spoor of dingoes and pademelons criss-cross the powdery snow. We follow the prints left by the rabbits, and the narrow granite walls echo our song in time to the jingling of the rusty traps:

'Run rabbit, run rabbit, run, run, run …'

Eagles circle and rabbits watch us pass with lichen dangling from their mouths. They waggle their long ears.

At the narrowest part of the track Billy hands me the first of the traps. I scoop a hole in the snow and bury the bulk of the metal, leaving just its jaws exposed, which I disguise with a light dusting of snow. We work our way back along the path until all the traps are laid. I bang the snow from my gloves and Billy hands me an onion sandwich from his satchel. I sit beside him on the trolley deck and we eat our lunch in comfortable silence. Now that the timber fellers have left Mount Delusion for the winter, there is no sound that doesn't belong here. I feel at peace, especially since the school teacher returned to Melbourne because Walter Cosgrove from the next valley died from catching measles, leaving only eight students, and that's not enough for the Department to keep paying for a part-time teacher.

I am sorry for little Walter though; of the other children who attended the school, he was the only one who did not make fun of me and Billy—nor laugh when the others called me 'horsie' or made neighing noises when I appeared with Billy on my back. Perhaps it was because Walter was also a weak boy. Perhaps it was because his father had left their house a year before to try his luck in the gold mines and had not returned.

'I'm cold, Lucy.'

I hadn't noticed Billy's lips turning blue. I gulp the last of my sandwich and, removing my gloves, put them over Billy's and rub his legs before rewrapping the blanket around his body.

'Hang on tight!' I call, and take off at a jog. Released from the weight of the traps, the trolley leaps forward. We sing to make the homeward trip shorter. Our singing gives way to uncontrollable giggles at the wobble in Billy's voice as he bounces over the rocks.

Tonight, his chesty cough fills our little home and I know I will have to collect the rabbits alone in the morning.

1935

A hot dry nor'easter sweeps across the mountains, sucking moisture from the air and from my skin. I peel flakes of loose skin from my lips, then curse as they sting and bleed. Summer also brings the horse flies. I pull a stiff frond of bracken and whip it across my back. The flies rise, then resettle, biting through my cotton shirt until the next swish. They buzz around my bare legs and my bare head.

I have grown taller than my parents and consider myself an adult; have done since the day I found blood trickling down my inner thighs and Ma handed me a square of towelling saying, 'Here, stick this in yer bloomers, you're a woman now'.

As I grow in strength, Billy grows weaker.

One day Dad comes home from the mill with a wheelchair strapped onto the side of his saddle—a fragile contraption with just a leather strip slung from a cane frame with two oversize wheels, but it is strong enough to hold Billy. Dad fits a ramp over the steps and, for the first time, Billy doesn't need me to carry him outside for a pee. Despite his new-found independence, I still piggy-back Billy into the forest where we sing our songs and scamper after wallabies. Mostly, though, I ride the mountains alone on Ginger, keeping watch on our cattle as they graze the summer grasses across Mount Delusion.

This morning, I raked the coals through the grate with care when I set the fire, selecting lumps of charcoal that clink in the bag dangling from my shoulder, for the drying winds of autumn produce a blank canvas for me to draw my pictures. Like snakes shedding last season's skin, the trees cast off last year's bark in long ribbons, exposing a pure cream trunk that feels cool and waxy to my touch.

At school, while the other children had drawn flat houses with pointed roofs, a central door flanked by two windows and stick men as tall as the house, I drew roads that snaked across fields, through a gate, and narrowed as they approached distant mountains to disappear within their folds. The schoolteacher would cluck about 'perspective'. I didn't understand, I simply drew life as I saw it, and the distant mountains were smaller than the gate before me.

Selecting a lump of charcoal with a fine point, I draw the outline of a lyrebird on the smooth trunk, accurately following, from memory, the outward curve of its feathers. Then I fill in each fine feather. I can't reproduce the body of the bird so easily. Its eye is all wrong. I smudge the eye, ruining the delicate work on the tail that has taken the best part of an hour. I move on to the next tree and, choosing a fresh piece of charcoal, begin again. This time, I leave a blank space for the bird's face—better an incomplete picture than one whose face doesn't fit.

Tree ferns are much easier; they don't contain faces that look at me accusingly if I can't capture their quirky ways. Again, with a fine point, I draw every division of every leaf then, with a rounded, softer piece of charcoal, shade beneath the fronds. It is so lifelike, the fern appears to be growing from the tree trunk as I stand back to admire my work.

*

Winter hits hard. The mill closes down and the loggers leave the mountain. For six months, despite failing health, Johnny toils around the house building a garden to grow vegetables, chopping a mountain of firewood for the coming winter, repairing the rabbit traps and taking Lucy into the bush to set the line. When he can achieve no more, he packs his saddlebag and joins so many other men on 'The Wallaby' in search of work figuring that, with one less mouth to feed, their families will survive till things improve.

A new year arrives, but Johnny does not return. Ella would like to know where her husband is. Summer turns to autumn, and Billy's already frail body shrinks with inactivity.

*

I pull on my gumboots and prepare to run the trap-line before the frost leaves the ground. Of the twenty traps I set, fifteen contain rabbits. I retrieve the trolley from the end of the line and work my way back, collecting my haul as I go. The small furry bodies glisten with frost as I slide a thin knife into the bellies and peel the skin from the bodies. I stretch fifteen skins on wire bows and gut the carcasses, then hang them in pairs from a wire between two tree trunks. I sit guard all day to chase the currawongs and crows.

Tonight, as the family feasts on rabbit stew, Billy's face grows pale and waxen, then he falls from his chair into a crumpled heap on the floor. I spring for the door without stopping to grab my coat and make for Ginger's shed and then ride, bareback, two miles to Uncle Jeff's farm. I open the door and run into the house, grabbing my uncle by the arm, pulling him towards the door.

'What's up Lucy? What's the panic?'

Billy's lying on the floor, he looks like he's dead!

Uncle Jeff can't make out my grunts, so he scrabbles around for a piece of paper and a stub of pencil.

'Here, write it.'

I scribble the words

I think Billy's dead

and thrust it into his hands.

'What is it?' Aunty Flo takes the paper from her husband then shows it to Grandma as Uncle Jeff rushes out to his horse. He and I gallop headlong back along Charlotte Spur Track.

Ma is on the floor, crying, with Billy's head in her lap, when we burst in. He has regained consciousness, but looks deathly white and his chest rattles with each shallow breath.

'Poor little bugger,' says Uncle Jeff. 'Hitch up the buggy, Ella, we've got to get him to the hospital.' Jeff lifts the featherweight of Billy; I throw his coloured rug over his legs.

*

I climb into the forest high on Dingo Ridge behind my hut. There, among familiar trees, I check the line of rabbit traps I have set and mourn the little boy whose legs have been stolen by polio and whose life has been robbed by influenza. I tell the lyrebirds of my misery, and they listen from the moist gully then give voice to their own secrets in carefully rendered verses: the howling of the dingoes; the ringing of the axe—but the timber-getters have not yet returned to Mount Delusion.

I climb further to an overhanging rock that only I know about and, on hands and knees, crawl over the soft powdered earth to the very back of a cave where daylight barely reaches. I curl into the curve of the rock face and, quietly crying, drift into a sleep filled with dreams of Billy. He has been my only means of communication beyond the animals and trees. Ma and I have little to say to each other and my father is still wandering the track unaware that his son has died.

It is after dark the following day when I return to my mother's fire. No sooner do I walk in than Ma turns on me, consumed with anger.

'Where have you been, girl? It's not enough that your father has deserted us, that your sister no longer wants to live here and your brother has chosen to die, now you wander off without so much as a word. I need you here. How am I supposed to cope on me own? You're a heartless soul. Your animals obviously mean more to you than your own family.'

I refuse to acknowledge the tears burning the back of my eyes as Ma slaps two plates on the table. We sit in silence and eat our rabbit stew.

*

As days become warmer and the axemen return to the mountain, I round up our thirty head of cattle and drive them onto the mountain to graze the summer grasses. I steer the mob along the wheel ruts halfway up to where the men have been working. The track is steep and rocky, but much easier for the cattle than the northern slopes cut by deep ravines. The sight of jagged trunks standing taller than a man surrounded by fallen branches makes my heart ache. I clamber onto a stump six feet across and sing mournful songs to their ghosts. Not a bird can be heard in the forest.

When I reach the top of Mount Delusion, the cattle fan out, heads down, grazing. I ride home to the thunder of Ma's words and I know I need to escape. I have grown used to a lifetime of aggression from her, but this new level of anger frightens me and I know I cannot be the companion she so desperately needs.

The next morning I rise and light the fire as usual, fill the kettle, collect the eggs and prepare breakfast, but instead of waiting for Ma to emerge from her bed, pinning her plait to the top of her head, I collect tins of stew and powdered milk, load them into Ginger's saddlebag, and ride west to the mountain to live with the cattle until oncoming winter will force us back down.

Keeping well clear of the loggers working the southern slopes, I wind my way up the steep ridges of the northern side through broad-leafed forests, letting Ginger pick his own way among the loose rocks. The higher I climb, the more sparse the trees grow. When I reach a stand of wattle just below alpine ash that ring the summit I signal Ginger to stop. I take an axe from my saddlebag and drop a dozen trunks of equal size and strip the branches. I stand them in a semi-circle and draw the tops together, binding them with a tough vine. Using my axe, I remove large sheets of fibrous bark from the butts of the ash and weave them through the wattle. Next, I fill a hessian sack with bracken to make a bed, then gather rocks into a fire ring at the opening to my shelter.

With nightfall, I light my fire—to warm my tinned stew, to warm my body, and to ward off any animals—and I listen to sounds from the axemen's camp below. As shouting settles into singing, I join in their songs. I sleep that night to the snuffles of night animals instead of Ma's snoring.

*

Daylight withdraws from inside the hut and Ella closes her Bible and places it on the kitchen table. Outside, Pansy the house cow lows patiently for Lucy to relieve her discomfort and collect some milk. Ella places the kettle on the flames as they grow. Pansy rubs her bulk against the corner of the building and continues her pathetic lowing.

In the morning, Ella follows the narrow path beaten by Lucy's daily trips through the ferns to the water that flows to the hut. Johnny had dug it years ago to bring water from Sheep Station Creek to their property. She plunges the kettle into the water, fills it and hurries back. With unsure hands, she squeezes Pansy's swollen udder and milk squirts loudly into the metal bucket.

For the first time in her life, Ella is alone.

*

I ride on to the top of the mountain to check the cattle. The dry grass snaps beneath Ginger's hooves. Alone on the mountain, I am able to grieve for Billy at my own pace. I ride through the trees or across the snowgrass fields, still feeling his arms wrapped around my waist, teasing me, encouraging me to gallop at full pelt till our faces grow red from windburn. I howl, long and loud into the night, like a dingo.

Days turn to weeks. When my supplies run low, I use my rifle to bring down a roo or a rabbit. I graze on soft fresh bracken fronds and wattle seeds. I carefully select the right pieces of charcoal to draw beautiful pictures on the pale trunks, not worrying that they will fade with the first fall of rain.

One day, while riding the top, I notice the air growing icy cold. For a few moments I feel relief from the scorching wind that has swept the mountaintop for the past four weeks robbing the snowgrass of any moisture, baking its blades brittle. Then I hear a roar building, drumming towards me. Ginger hears it too and his hide quivers beneath my legs. Some of the cattle fanning across the mountain, their red-brown rumps to the wind, lift their heads to test the threat, lowing lazily then bow their heads and continue to graze.

As the blue-green belly of the storm clouds drop their icy load into the valley below, I ride around the thirty head of cattle steering them down to the protection of the ash forest. The sting of hail and the flash of lightning quickens the cattle and I bend flat along Ginger's back as he thunders, snorting, between the trunks. The clouds slide over the remaining daylight, turning the bark high on the ash from white to mauve. With the cattle safely among the trees, I dismount and lead Ginger to shelter behind the largest of the trunks and pull my oilskin from the saddlebag.

Sleet follows the hail, slicing the air, engulfing, freezing everything in its path. The wind's scream obliterates all other sounds as ice crystals settle on top of my black gumboots for a moment, then melt. I shake my foot and the drops join to trickle from my boot. Sleet stings my cheeks and forces its way inside my upturned collar.

The temperature plummets further and curtains of ice give way to scurrying snowflakes that patter more gently upon my head.

Billy would have flicked the snowflakes from my shoulder-length hair he said reminded him of summer straw.

And still the wind screams, whipping tall straight trunks of the ash as if they were saplings. From deep within the forest comes the sound of thunder then splitting wood after lightning blows the heart out of an old tree. I hug my coat close to my waist, feeling the trapped warmth against my skin. Icy water drips from my trousers into my boots.

After half an hour the storm passes to the south-east, leaving a musty smell of wet earth—it smells like the dirt they shovelled over Billy—and a coating of snow over everything. Yellow-tailed black cockatoos circle the valley, filling it with their eerie call. It is not yet May, but the arrival of the snow signals the end of summer freedom for the cattle. And for me.

Little light remains in the sky when I reach my lean-to. I remove the saddle from Ginger and wipe his coat clean of dirt and snow before turning him loose. I light the fire at the entrance of my small shelter and empty my last tin of stew into a battered saucepan to balance it on the crackling fire. Billy would have stirred it with a fork to make sure it didn't stick on the bottom.

I didn't think it was possible to miss someone as much as I miss him.

The meal warms my belly as I lie down to stare into the fire and drift off to sleep with the sighing of the trees. Here I find escape from the incessant chatter of my mother and her never-ending list of chores. With the passing of the storm, I know the time has come to round up the cattle and head down to the farm, and Ma.

The cattle, sensing the change of season, come easily when I drop clumps of salt on the ground and call to them—'S-a-a-a-alt'. Again, I choose the loggers' track, as the descent is much smoother than my horse trail. I ride slowly, taking care not to spook the beasts; to allow them to set their own pace along the rock-strewn ridge that drops away hundreds of feet to my right. I look out across ridge after ridge dusted with snow, and the land begins to heal my soul.

At the bottom of the descent, I leave the cattle free to roam among the trees—I will brand the calves later—but overriding the forest noises comes the sound of sawing and hammering. Approaching my hut, I am confronted by utter confusion. Half a dozen men, under the direction of Uncle Jeff, crawl over the framework of a new structure that hides our bark and tin hut from view. Stacks of milled timber lie around. Sheets of roofing tin lean against a tree, and watching every saw-cut and hammer-blow, hands on hips, stands Ma. At the sound of a snort from Ginger she turns, face beaming, and smiles up at me.

'Uncle Jeff reckons we need a new place, Lucy. How do you like it?'

I dismount, stunned, and walk through a doorway in the front wall and enter the two rooms—a bedroom and a living room, complete with a fireplace. Everyone pauses, waiting for my reaction. I cannot comprehend this change in my home, nor in my mother; it is as if she is trying to expunge all memory of our past.

Why now? When there is just you and me?

I come out of the new building and face my mother, my face red with rage and frustration at not being able to speak the truth— *This can never be our home.*

I mount Ginger and ride back to the familiarity of my lean-to on Mount Delusion.

1938

Red mud flicks from the iron wheels of the old cane pram, freckling Ella's sturdy legs as she leans into the handle bar, pushing the pram along the track to Carroll's farm. Each step she takes adds another layer of clay to the soles of her boots until her calves ache with the effort of lifting them. And the pram is yet to be filled with the week's groceries.

Without Lucy trudging beside her, the three miles to Carroll's farm stretches interminably, giving Ella way too much time to think. For nineteen years she has put up with Lucy's stubborn silences along with unintelligible outbursts that spring from nowhere. They have been easily absorbed as part of the web of family life within the towering gums of the Victorian High Country. Half a dozen families dot the logging track passing through the Brookville district, each too busy eking out a living to spend time chewing the fat. The men, mostly employed at the local mill, do not discuss family life.

Jessie Carroll is standing at her farmhouse door, arms akimbo, as Ella pushes the pram across her front paddock.

'Kettle's on,' she calls in welcome.

Ella leaves the pram and her boots by the steps and follows Jessie into the front room, removing her hat and patting her hair into place. The two women sit at the kitchen table either side of the teapot.

'Has Lucy come back?' asks Jessie.

Ella shakes her head. Sips her tea.

'I don't know where she's gone, or how long she'll be.'

'I reckon she's gone mad,' offers Jessie. 'Doctor Freeman says the best thing is to get her checked out. If she is mad, then the place for her is in hospital.' She takes another sip of tea.

Ella's first reaction is one of anger over the possibility that others have been discussing her affairs behind her back, but slowly she begins to see that maybe this is an explanation for her daughter's erratic behaviour. By the time she has loaded her pram with the weekly shopping order and mail Tom Carroll had brought on horseback from Swifts Creek, she is almost convinced that this is the case.

*

Winter returns with bitter nights and cold days and I once more have my mountain to myself. I set Ginger free to return to the farm; this is no place for a horse any more than it is for a nineteen-year-old woman, but I have ways of dealing with such extreme living. Skins of rabbits and kangaroos to strengthen my shelter. Fires to keep me warm.

When the days finally begin to warm and the snows melt, I make my way down the steep slopes and return home ready, once again, to face life with Ma.

The new dwelling stands, lifeless, before the old hut. It turns out that even Ma can't adjust to change. I take up my seat at the table by the old fireplace and wait for Ma to bring my dinner, as if I have never been away, but without so much as a word of welcome, Ma runs out the door, down the track heading for Carroll's farm. Something about the look on her face causes fear to creep up my spine and I leave the table for the safety of Dingo Ridge.

*

Tree trunks cast their late-afternoon shadows across the lush, moist undergrowth. In the stillness within the forest, not a leaf stirs. Small birds busy themselves in pursuit of their evening meal. A wallaby wakes from its daytime nap and stands erect, testing the air with a twitching nose, then drops onto its front paws and moves off to nibble the freshly opened crosiers of giant tree ferns. A lyrebird works its way through its repertoire, unseen, from a moist gully.

A black vehicle pulls into the track beside Strobridge's huts. A police sergeant and Doctor Freeman emerge from the front and Ella from the back.

*

Crouched low among the ferns, I watch, my every sense alert for the tell-tale crack of a twig, or the tread of feet across leaf litter. My calves ache from squatting on the steep slope, and I wriggle my bare feet in the soft mulch to ease the strain on my ankles, releasing a heady mix of musty earth and eucalypt. Far below the forest, where the mountainside is not so steep, I can hear the raspy voice of Ma calling me, but I know I'm safe; she won't venture into the bush on Dingo Ridge.

A breeze stirs and the leaves part. Far below, Ma paces backwards and forwards, waving her arms, calling to me to come down. No-one is going to hurt me, she says. I don't believe my mother—not with the police car parked on the side of the road in front of the hut, its rear door open, waiting to swallow me.

I hear other voices, closer now, as the police officer and Doctor Freeman call my name, passing in and out of the shadows of tree trunks below. I can tell they are unused to climbing mountains, the way they lean forward, grasping for any sapling or clump of fern, unable to get purchase on the long smooth leaves dropped by the manna gums. By the time they have covered half the distance between my mother and me, I can hear their laboured breathing as they call my name.

'Lucy!'

Do you really think I'll answer you?

I slip silently from my hiding place and continue higher up the slope, keeping the thickest trunks and the tallest ferns between myself and my pursuers, making for the overhanging rock near Dingo Ridge track. I am certain no-one else knows of this rock. I have spent many nights camped on its floor of fine dust, and each time I return, the hessian sack stuffed with fern that I use as a mattress remains undisturbed. When I reach the rock, I crawl to the very back of the overhang where it is dim and safe.

Half an hour passes, then the faint light at the entrance to my small cave darkens with the bulk of the doctor bending over. The saliva dries in my mouth.

'Now Lucy, don't be afraid.'

I smell his sweat; I'm sure he smells my fear as I press into the hard rock and open my throat wide in a scream. The policeman crawls past the doctor and reaches out to me. I bite down hard on his hand and scratch at his face.

'You're a wild one, aren't you,' he says, grabbing my feet and pulling. For all my strength, I can't fight off the two men as they drag me, slipping and sliding, down the mountainside. We reach the hut and, for a moment, Ma and I lock eyes. I see how she fears my wildness. She turns and runs towards the hut, calling over her shoulder, 'Take her, just take her,' unable to watch as the two men push me into the rear seat of the police car.

*

Lucy's screams hang in Ella's ears long after the car disappears. Ella reaches for her Bible and opens it randomly, reading aloud to cleanse the screams from her ears.

Ella cannot focus on the text as Lucy's face, twisted in panic, floats across the small black print. She flicks the delicate, well-thumbed pages, searching for a passage that will justify her actions. The closest she can find is in the book of Proverbs:

> Do not hold back discipline from the mere boy. In case you beat him with the rod, he will not die. With the rod you yourself should beat him, that you may deliver his very soul from Sheol itself.

Surely she could be forgiven for wishing to save her daughter from Death?

*

I fix my eyes on the caged light bulb directly overhead. All around are unfamiliar noises. A car horn penetrates the brick walls of the Bairnsdale General Hospital. I flinch and the woman in the next bed stops counting momentarily, then resumes until she reaches twenty. Always twenty. She whispers her numbers so she won't disturb the other people in the receiving ward, all awaiting the superintendent's pleasure to be classified as sane or insane.

Stop it, you stupid woman!

Across the ward, a young woman sings to herself. I can't distinguish the words or the tune.

At least you have a nice voice.

Thoughts race around my brain, but none form into words. I continue staring at the off-white ceiling, absorbing the foreignness, feeling very frightened. Occasionally a door opens, disturbing the air, but what I notice most are the sounds I cannot hear: the scratching of the bush rat in the wood box beside the firepit; the eerie cry of the yellow-tailed black cockatoo lazily flapping along the valley in search of pine cones; the scraping of coarse hide on floor bearers as the wombat arches its back, eyes closed in bliss, to rub an itchy spot it can't reach; Pansy, calling for me to draw her milk.

I strain against the coarse cloth that pins my aching arms and numbs my fingers. A nurse pads around the scrubbed floor, eternally fussing. Her white-capped head bends over me, blocking the light from the bare bulb as she lifts my head, plumping the pillow, and reinserting it. She tucks the blanket around my legs. I kick it off, grunting at renewed efforts to free myself from the straightjacket.

'Don't be a naughty girl!' The nurse frowns.

I'm not a girl! I'm a woman!

An hour passes, and the nurse returns with a bowl of stew.

'If you promise not to throw your food at the wall again, Lucy, I will let you feed yourself.'

I soften the look in my eyes and nod, and the nurse unties the straightjacket, releasing my hands. As I pump my fingers, the blood returns, painfully. Hunger forces me to accept the meal that I have refused over the past three days. It tastes salty, but I gulp it down.

'Good girl. Now, are you going to behave?'

Again I nod as I hand the empty bowl to the nurse and settle into bed to stare at the light. Thick brick walls maintain the air at a constant temperature. Night feels the same as day. This is unnatural. From the next bed, the counting is so soft, I have to strain my ears to hear:

'One, two, three, four, five, six, seven, eight, nine, ten, eleven, twelve, thirteen, fourteen, fifteen, sixteen, seventeen, eighteen, nineteen, twenty …'

The nurse flicks out the light and in the darkness the soft voice brings comfort as I drift away to my mountains; to a time before Billy died.

*

I wake with a start as a car backfires somewhere outside. Every fibre in my being screams, reaching my throat. Footsteps pound along the ward; strong arms grab me; I feel a needle in my arm; my ears buzz and my eyes swim; blackness envelops my world.

I wake to a distant voice, 'The doctor wants to see you now, Lucy'. I go to rise from my bed but find my arms bound once again, my fingers as numb as my brain. A man in a white coat lifts me to my feet and steers me through a long corridor to a room with a large wooden table. He guides me into a hard upright chair opposite another man with wire-rimmed spectacles whose downcast eyes scan a sheet of white paper. Minutes pass, and he eventually looks up at me, removing his spectacles.

'Is it necessary for her to be restrained?' he asks the wardsman.

'She's a feisty one. We're never sure when she'll lash out.'

'Be that as it may, I think she is sedated enough for you to remove the restraint.'

The wardsman remains, hands clasped behind his back, standing beside my chair. The doctor rises and approaches me, perching on the corner of the table, peering into my eyes.

'Lucy'—he speaks slowly, as if to a child—'if you promise you will behave, I will untie your arms'.

I nod. He upholds his promise. I spring from the chair and dash towards the door, straight into the arms of the wardsman who clamps my hands behind my back.

'Now Lucy,' says the doctor, 'I don't think that's fair. You promised to behave'. He sees the fear in my eyes as I twist my head towards the wardsman.

'Would you prefer he isn't here?'

Again, I nod.

'Would you please leave us alone? I will take full responsibility for any repercussions.'

The wardsman releases his grasp and disappears through the door and locks it before I can react. I look wildly around the room, searching for an escape. The doctor walks to his side of the desk and motions to the chair in front of him. It is the first time I notice that he has a limp and kind eyes. I sit on the edge of the chair and face him.

'Lucy, I know you can't speak, but is there anything you would like to tell me?'

I shake my head.

'Doctor Freeman says your mother is worried that you are not in control of your actions. What do you say to that?'

Mention of my mother brings rage to my eyes. I scream. The door flings open and my arms are once again clamped by the wardsman's huge hands. The doctor rises and closes my file.

'We'll talk later, when you have had time to calm down. I do want to help you, but unless we can discuss things, I'm afraid you will have to stay restrained.'

Back in my bed, my arms pinioned, I listen again to the relentless counting: 'One, two, three, four …'

*

The next time I sit before the doctor there is a sheet of paper and a pencil on my side of the desk. The doctor unties the ties, releasing my arms.

'What do you want, Lucy? What would make you happy?'

I pick up the pencil and write one word:

Billy

'Who's Billy?'

my brother

'Where is Billy?'

in the ground

'Did Billy die?'

Tears sting my eyes. I wipe them with the back of my hand. The doctor closes the file in front of him.

'I don't think you are insane, Lucy. I think you are in grief.'

*

The third time the doctor opens his door to admit me I stand, stunned by the sight of my father—a shadow of the man I had last seen four years before—sitting in the chair I normally occupy, staring at the floor, his elbows resting on his knees. My father is not a well man. The doctor welcomes me then leaves the room.

I remember all the times we shared in the forest: the lessons on how to set rabbit traps; which trees were best to ringbark; the touch needed to sharpen an axe on the slab of rock. The gentle way he used to carry Billy.

Dad remains slouched in his chair, head bowed, gripping his pipe between his teeth, shuffling the brim of his hat through his hands. It is only when he feels my hand rest on his shoulder that he raises his head, revealing haunted red-rimmed eyes. Eventually, he clears his throat and speaks in little more than a whisper, straining to keep his voice even.

'Tom Carroll sent me a letter. Told me what your ma had done. Truth is, Lucy, I reckon they took the wrong one away. It should have been her. You're no more mad than I am.'

He stands. 'Get yer things, we're going home.'

Doctor Freeman drives my father and me back to our home in Brookville. Without a second thought, I open the door to the house built by Uncle Jeff and claim it as my own.

Within the year, they bury my father in the Omeo Cemetery. He is just fifty-two.

1939

The giant quivers from its canopy to its almost-severed butt seventy feet below as the axemen drive home the wedges. It teeters then, with the crack of splitting wood, begins its fall to the forest floor. Slowly at first, its branches supported by neighbouring trees, then with gathering speed until it lands on outstretched limbs and bounces as if on a spring. Only when it has stopped all movement do Arty and Bob approach with, as always, a sense of awe. They top it, then systematically work along the log, removing limbs, each one as thick as a tree, all the time being buzzed by horse flies.

Arty hears the snort of two horses and the clank of the snigger's chain being laid out along the ground in readiness. They finish stripping the log and signal for Alex to hitch the horses to the log. The huge log moves more readily as it gains momentum, easing the strain on the horses, allowing them to set a rhythm as he walks beside. Not to guide them—they know the path to the tramline well— but to secure the log onto the bogies of the tram below the earthen ramp.

He hitches the horses to the front and climbs onto the log, looping a length of rope from the brake lever around his arm in readiness for the six-mile descent to the mill at Brookville. Normally, Arty and Bob would set fire to the dropped crown to encourage the seeds to begin their journey to become forest giants of the future, but this year the air is so dry they dare not risk the inevitable fire that would race through the tinder-dry canopy. Word has spread that a huge fire is burning out of control to the north, threatening the whole of the Victorian bush.

They clean their axes and take turns on the handle of the grindstone to sharpen the blades. Arty brushes his calloused thumb across the edge, checking for burrs and only when he is satisfied does he grease the blade and pack it away in its box. He is square and solid, and although only 22 years of age, is a veteran logger. Bob, five years younger but with a build equal to Arty's, lifts the billy from the fire and pours two mugs of strong tea, then sits on the log beside Arty. The two men drink in silence in the stump-spiked clearing. Beyond the clearing a wall of trees, each twelve feet across at the ground, stands waiting—next year's harvest. They have finished logging this coupe. Tomorrow they will pack up their tents and move to the next patch.

'And good riddance to the bloody flies!' says Arty, whose bare arms are covered in red welts.

For the past four months the logging gang has camped in six-foot square canvas tents erected in a semi-circle around the mess tent, surrounded by alpine ash—or woolly butt, as they call it—preferring to camp near the coupe rather than ride down the steep overgrown track to the mill houses each evening and return the next morning.

They form a close bond on the mountain. Each man knows his job and is respected by the others: the fallers, the sniggers, the men who ride the bogies down the wooden tramline to the mill, the teams of horses—unlike the drifters who work for a short time at the mill. The regulars cannot respect them.

With the log on its way down the mountain, the rest of the men gather for their last meal before striking camp.

'They reckon the fires are headed this way,' says Bob.

'I can't see how. They're burning up along the Murray. They would need to jump across Hotham to reach us, and I reckon that's impossible.'

'Still, I'd be surprised if we aren't pulled out altogether until they're sure.'

At first light the next morning, they take down their tents and load them onto drays to begin the long descent to Brookville, passing two huts set back among the trees. Arty wonders what the two women who live in them will do if the fire comes this way.

Arty and Bob ride on to Swifts Creek as the sun sets with an eerie orange glow that barely penetrates the smoke fogging their township. Ted Worthing, a local farmer and bush fireman, sees them ride in and urgently waves them over. Dressed in a heavy woollen overcoat, he is bathed in perspiration.

'It's jumped Hotham and taken out most of Omeo!'

'Jesus! It must be an almighty fire!' says Arty.

'The Omeo hospital's gone,' shouts Ted.

'Was anyone killed?' asks Arty.

'No, but it was a close call. Matron watched the fire burn other buildings and as it headed towards the hospital, she went to start her car to get the patients out, but it was so hot, the damn thing wouldn't start. She even prepared morphine for the patients at one stage, in case they couldn't escape, but then she poured water over the engine to cool it and they all got away. Any later and it would

have been curtains.' He points across the road to the pub. 'She's brought them here to the Albion.'

Arty and Bob jump into the back of the fire truck beside the water tank, and three more men join them.

'I really don't know what we can do,' says Ted as he puts the truck into gear and crawls off along the road towards the flames that are now clearly visible above the trees.

They return at midnight to defend their own houses and shops. Spot fires spring up all around town as embers are carried through the air on a hot northerly wind. The firemen race from one small fire to the next, beating the flames with wet sacks before they can take hold in the parched grass. They turn their hose on a blaze behind Slater's cafe, then a flaming branch settles behind Sandy's shop against the drums of his petrol store. Five thousand gallons explode in a giant fireball. Dawn arrives with the firemen still fighting.

'Has the fire reached Brookville?' Arty asks Ted.

'Not yet. It swung east when it topped Hotham, through Omeo, then south to here.'

Arty looks to Bob and smiles with relief. They are both thinking the same thing: at least their precious forest is safe for now, and so are the two women living on the slopes of Mount Delusion. By mid-afternoon the wind drops then slowly builds from the south. The horrific fire stops in its path and turns on itself, but there is little bush left to burn.

*

I can smell smoke. It must be behind the mountain, because that's where the wind is blowing from. I walk out from my hut as darkness is falling and the sky is a murky orange. It's like a sunset, only the sun doesn't set in the north. I feel the hair prickle on the back of my neck. We are so vulnerable living in the middle of the forest. So are the animals.

Ma appears in her doorway; she has smelt it too. She looks at me with fear in her eyes.

'We are safe, aren't we Lucy?' It is a question I cannot answer.

I return to my bedroom and crawl beneath my blankets. Sometime through the night, I feel vibrations through my mattress as the air is buffeted by explosions. I jump and run outside and the orange glow of earlier is now so intense it looks like an early dawn, so I run up the hill to see. Smoke fills the valleys in orange pools. Above the trees on the road to Swifts Creek, a ball of flames soars into the sky.

At the first hint of daylight I mount Ginger and ride along Brookville Road towards Swifts Creek to see for myself what is happening. As I reach the crest of the hill above the township the bush changes from green to black so suddenly it takes my breath away. The gravel road winds its way starkly through still-smouldering tree trunks. I can feel the heat on my legs as I ride on, expecting to find nothing remaining of the shops and houses of Swifts Creek. Then I enter green again. The little town sits safely within a circle that has been saved.

*

For seven days the firemen follow the fire, joining other fire trucks from other districts, making sure the fire is contained and saving what they can. But mills have burnt, houses have burnt, people have died. The Victorian High Country has changed irrevocably.

*

I ride home to where I live in my hut and Ma lives in hers—two women living so near, yet make little attempt at contact. Each morning I empty Ma's night bucket, fill the kettle, collect the eggs, milk Pansy. I set the fire for the day as Ma's hut is where all the cooking is done, but I don't eat with her. We have little to say to each other. Each time I look at her, I remember that she sent me away. I cannot forgive her for that.

She cooks my meal and delivers it to me. I mostly pretend I don't hear her knock on my door, so she leaves my plate on the doorstep. When I hear her moving about in her hut, I sneak open my door and retrieve the plate. If I have been rabbiting and left the carcasses hanging on a wire by her door, it is rabbit stew, otherwise she warms up tins of Irish Stew. Never one for cooking more than is necessary, her standards have slipped even further. It is as if she has given up on life.

Winter brings snow and a relief from the threat of bushfires, but I have grown anxious whenever I smell smoke that isn't of my own making, and I hate riding through burnt out forests where no animals live.

Spring brings surprises with it. Although the ground is still grey, thick with ash, tiny green shoots appear. I have seen this before. It takes the heat of such an intense fire to give life to thousands of seeds from the old trees. So there is hope. I am careful where Ginger places his hooves so we don't trample this new life.

I drive the cattle along the track to the top of the mountain. They belong to Uncle Jeff now—he took over the herd after Dad died—but I still take them for their summer grazing on the southern side of the mountain where the fire did not reach. I love the freedom of living on the mountain in my shelter. I refresh the bark on the outside and inside, I replace the bracken in my sleeping mat. Life is simple and uncomplicated up among the alpine ash and snow gums.

I hear the loggers in the distance, but their noise is different this year. Instead of the thud of axes and the crash of trees coming to earth, there is the sound of an engine and a blast of a whistle.

1941

*B*ob *wraps leather leggings around his shins and fastens the strap beneath his boots, making sure the spurs sit snug against his inside anklebones. He walks, feet spread apart so he doesn't tangle the spurs, to the foot of the woolly butt and looks straight up two hundred feet. In his nineteen years, he doesn't remember feeling such exhilaration, or such fear. From his waist, a one-man crosscut saw dangles free. He pushes it towards his back to give him room.*

Arty takes the weight of the saw as Bob wraps a leather belt from his waist around the tree and buckles it firmly. He becomes part of the tree. Lifting the belt as high as possible, he bends his left leg and embeds the spike into the trunk. He pushes against the spike and his right foot draws level with his left. His temples throb, his mouth is dry. He leans into the tree and, with one smooth action, loosens the grip of the belt from around the giant trunk and tosses it as high as it will go, then left foot; right foot. He no longer looks up the trunk. He knows he will be climbing for the best part of an hour before reaching the crown and he needs to hold his nerve.

The higher he climbs the more he can see of what was once a mighty forest sloping away to the north. Now, the side of the mountain bristles with bare woolly butt trunks. Such is the nature of these trees that they will not reshoot like most eucalypts. That is why he is risking his life to reach the top of this particular tree. Unlike the dead trees below that are only good for the timber that can be salvaged, this tree, untouched by the fire, is a living being and will make a good spar tree to attach the high lead lines which, powered by a steam winch, will haul log after log from out of the ravine.

The Forests Commission has ordered that all loggers focus on salvaging as much of the burnt ash as possible before it rots into the ground. The owners of the sawmills that haven't been lost in the fire have bought steam winches and towed them into the forests on skids. The mountain slope is too steep to get the burnt timber out any other way. With the winch positioned at the top of this unburnt ridge, the loggers will be able to haul up logs from way down the slope.

Needing a source of water to feed the boilers, the men have dammed a spring that flows out from the granite rocks, forming a pond large enough for them to bathe in each evening, a luxury they have not had at any other camp. While they were at it, they dug a hole into the side of the mountain, shored up the walls and roof with sections of tree trunks, and made a walkway from pipe and galvanised iron that zigzags into the opening in the hope of preventing flames entering the space. Building such a dugout is one of the Commission's rules they must obey if they still want to work deep in the forests since the horrific fires of '39.

After forty minutes of steady climbing, Bob reaches the first of the branches to be removed. Leaning back against the leather belt, he swings the saw into position and cuts through branch after branch until only the crown remains. It is thirsty work at any time, but nearly two hundred feet up the tree, with the wind picking up, his mouth is so dry he can't swallow.

Before the final cut, he looks down to where Arty is waiting, his neck gone numb from continually looking up. Behind Arty, the men are patiently waiting by the steam winch, ready to play their role in the salvage process.

'It's now or never,' Bob says aloud. He turns the saw on its side and begins the final cut to remove the crown. He has been warned to hang on for dear life once the top lets go, and the men know what they are talking about. Relieved of its load, the trunk thrashes like a wild beast as Bob hangs on for the ride of his life, unable to stop the loud whoops that fly, involuntarily, from his mouth. It seems like forever, but eventually the arc of the sweep lessens and the tree comes to rest with a shudder as Bob begins the slow climb back to earth. Right foot down, dig in spur, left foot down, dig in spur, pull belt down.

He lands beside Arty three hours after he had left, and collapses into the soft ferns at the foot of the giant, unable to stand after the strain of digging his spurs into the trunk. His calf muscles threaten to cramp as he lies back and closes his eyes; nothing in life could equal this experience.

Arty bends over Bob, holding out the waterbag. He taps him on the shoulder, 'Here mate, you look like you could do with a drink'.

Bob props himself up on one elbow and drinks deeply.

'Bloody hell, that was something,' he says, wiping his mouth with the back of a hand covered in fine sawdust.

Arty laughs. 'Glad you liked it. You'll be up there again tomorrow to set up the pulley, but we'll call it a day for now.' He offers Bob a hand and pulls him from his nest in the tree ferns.

While Arty and Bob are preparing the spar tree, the rest of the logging gang work below, clearing a path down to the area they will be working tomorrow.

That night, the men camp in a clearing by the winch.

*

'Come on matey, time to stir yourself.' Arty leans across the gap between the two camp stretchers and shakes Bob's arm, hanging limp over the edge. It takes three prods before Bob stirs, groans, and rolls over. Every muscle aches, and he hasn't slept more than an hour at a stretch without his legs cramping.

'I can't,' he groans.

'Yes you can. You're young.'

'You're only five years older than me,' he complains. 'Can't you do it?'

'I would if I could, but they've decided you are the best climber to do the rigging, and I have to agree with them.'

Bob slowly pulls himself up on his stretcher, arms resting on his knees, his dark curly hair all a-tangle. Secretly, he is flattered that he has been chosen and he is very aware that his reputation has jumped from being the young'un to being the rigger. He reaches for his trousers, then straps the leggings onto his calves. Breakfast is a hurried affair; he is eager to begin the climb again and get the job finished.

This time, instead of a saw hanging from the rings riveted to his belt, he attaches a light pulley and length of rope. Two hundred feet up doesn't seem so high today, and when he attaches the pulley to the top of the spar, he feeds the rope through and returns it to the men waiting on the ground. By noon, most of the gear has been hauled up for Bob to firmly attach to the top, then comes a box with some sandwiches. He makes himself comfortable in a rope chair and eats his lunch with his feet dangling over the ravine.

'This has got to be the best view in the world to eat lunch.' He grins, enjoying a privilege that is his alone.

When he is sure all is secure enough to haul a huge log eight hundred yards up a very steep slope, he lowers himself, steadied by the ground men, down to earth in the rope chair.

Alex takes up his post at the winch, feeding the fire to get the boiler up to pressure as the rest of the gang walk down into the gully and manhaul the mainline chain to the first of the fallen woolly butt. They attach the collar securely around the butt of the trunk, then Arty pulls on a line that leads back to a steam whistle on the winch. Three blasts—'go ahead on the main line, slowly'. Four blasts when the log snags on a stump—'slack the main line,' then three blasts again. When light begins to fade, Arty gives five blasts, signalling an end to logging for the day.

*

Towards summer's end it becomes obvious that salvaging from the mountainside will take more than one season, so the men haul milled timber up from Brookville mill and take time out to build themselves a two-roomed hut. They might as well spend the logging season in comfort. Now, in the chill of the evenings, they sit around a fireplace instead of a campfire. They miss the stars, but not the mud and rain

1948

I wake to the sound of the wombat returning to its burrow. My sleep has been filled with dreams of escaping a bushfire so fierce I can feel the heat on my face. I lie looking at the ceiling which Uncle Jeff had papered with the same wallpaper as the walls. It sags where the hessian lining has come away from the rafters and wafts in the breeze floating through gaps in the walls. When I rise, I realise the fire is in my jaw. I place my hand to my cheek; even the gentlest of pressures causes my tooth to throb, churning my stomach.

I change into my day clothes and cross the open ground to my mother's hut to attend to her bucket and set the cooking fire. She is fussing about the place, sweeping the dirt floor with a fresh ti-tree broom she has made. She looks up as I enter and I see alarm on her face. She rushes towards me with her hand raised. She turns the back of her hand towards my face and I flinch, afraid she is about to strike me, but her hand comes to rest gently on my forehead.

'My God, girl, you're burning up!'

I pull her hand away. She touches my cheek and I nearly faint.

'Open up, and give me a look.'

I open my mouth; the pain increases. Ma gently inserts her index finger and massages my swollen gum.

'We've got to get you to the dentist. Have a Bex, and we'll see if Mr Carroll can take us to Swifts Creek in time to catch the mail van.'

Before the headache powder has a chance to dull the pain, Ma marches me up the track to Carroll's farm, walking straight into their hallway without knocking on the front door.

Squashed into the front seat of the truck between Ma and Mr Carroll, I wince as each bump in the road sends bolts of pain through my jaw. Mr Carroll points to the blue-black clouds in the north: 'I don't like the look of them. It'll snow before the day's out'.

We pull up at Swifts Creek store just as the contractor is walking to his van to take the mail to Bairnsdale. Ma pushes me forward, saying: 'You've got to help us. Lucy needs to get to the dentist'.

The contractor, a local from Swifts Creek, opens the passenger door for me to climb into the sole passenger seat.

'Here you go young lady, hop up and we'll get you to the dentist.'

He turns to Ma.

'I'll look after Lucy, Mrs Strobridge, you needn't worry. And I'll wait and bring her back when she's finished.'

Ma returns home in Carroll's truck, trusting I will be able to see the dentist today.

I wind the window fully open, despite a crisp wind. The chill air brings some relief to the fire in my cheek. The contractor tries to engage me in conversation, but I have no desire to communicate, even if I could. After twenty minutes, he gives up and concentrates on the winding dirt road. I lean my head against the pillar and close my eyes. It is a long drive, over an hour, and every bump increases my pain. I doze fitfully, only waking to the creak of the handbrake.

'Here we are Lucy. Do you want me to come with you?'

I know this place well. Ma and I share a passion for healthy teeth and we visit each year—but this time my mother is not here to speak for me. I nod acceptance and the contractor opens my door and walks with me into the dentist's surgery. As the receptionist shepherds me through to the room, the contractor says, 'I'll call back for her in an hour'.

The dentist places a gas mask over my nose. I feel its smooth roundness against my cheeks, smell the strong smell of rubber, then gas, then nothing. When the dentist next speaks, it is as if no time has elapsed, and I panic at the thought of being conscious before he has seen to my tooth. I run my tongue over my teeth and it rests in a gap where there has been a tooth and I taste fresh blood.

'It's lucky you came when you did, Miss Strobridge, you had a nasty abscess on the root. It must have caused you a lot of pain.'

He hands me some pills.

'These should help. I put a couple of stitches in your gum, so you'll need to return at the end of the week for me to remove them. In the meantime, take it easy.'

In the waiting room, the mail contractor rises to meet me.

'All done?'

I nod and head for his van parked in the street. Again, I wind down the window and lean my head on the side of the car and close my eyes for the entire journey to Swifts Creek.

The sun has set by the time the mail van pulls to a stop outside Sandy's store. A group of men are gathered, chewing the fat, out front. Tall and lean, with a stoop from a lifetime of lugging bags of supplies into the back room of the store, Sandy walks with a measured gate. He wanders over to the van, opening the passenger door for me.

'No need to be in a hurry, Lucy, the road's blocked. Tom Carroll won't be able to get his truck out for a few days.'

He nods towards the Albion Hotel across the road.

'You'll have to stay there the night.'

Ted, the proprietor of the pub, joins Sandy and me on the footpath, rolling tobacco for a cigarette between his palms. He wraps a paper around the tobacco then places it between his lips and lights the end, waiting for it to glow before speaking.

'Tell you what Lucy: I need a hand in the kitchen. My regular got caught in the storm and can't get through from Waterfall. You can stay for free if you give us a hand. What do you say?'

I nod, and would have smiled had my painful mouth allowed. I follow Ted across the road. He leads me to a room out the back of the hotel and opens the door.

'Here you are love. Hope this'll do.'

The room is small, containing a single bed, a narrow wardrobe and a chair, but it has walls and a door. I notice the door has no lock but I don't worry; I will prop the chair under the door knob to make sure no drunks come in uninvited during the night. I nod twice in acceptance.

'The bathroom's out on the back verandah. You'll have to share it, we've got a couple of guests—which is why I need a hand. Come on, I'll show you to the kitchen.'

I follow Ted down the hallway into a kitchen complete with a rotund cook and dirty dishes. Cook is standing by a very large wood stove, stirring an equally large pot. I look in and see a rich broth brewing and the steam fills my nostrils, reminding me I haven't eaten at all today. On the back plate of the stove another large pot is just beginning to bubble with clear water. I roll my sleeves past my elbows and fill the sink with hot water, ignoring Cook standing by. I swish in suds and don't lift my head until the drainer is stacked with clean plates. When I am finished, Cook hands me a bowl of broth.

'Here love, I reckon you've earned this.' Then she adds, 'You don't talk much, do you'.

I smile and take the bowl, aware that my stomach is rumbling in readiness. I sit at a scrubbed-pine kitchen table and gingerly sip from the side of the spoon, avoiding my swollen gum. It tastes hot, salty and good.

As I lie down to sleep that night, it all feels so foreign, and I wonder if I have the courage to live with people who are not my family, but I can't dismiss the thrill I feel at the possibility. I miss the sound of the wombat leaving on its nightly patrol, but I don't miss the constant demands of my mother.

Cook taps on my door before daybreak. I open it a few inches and she holds out some clean underclothes and a shirt.

'They'll be miles too big for you, but you'll need something fresh to wear for the next couple of days. Come to the kitchen as soon as you can; the porridge needs stirring.'

I smile my thanks and go to the bathroom to bathe and dress.

*

Days pass and the snow melts. Cook seems to accept the fact that I don't talk and she gives me chores that keep me busy: preparing vegetables; cleaning lettuce for salads; dicing beef for her famous stew. She says she is very pleased with the way I do these things without any fuss or carry on. They are the same chores Ma asks of me, but Cook has a way of asking instead of telling, and she always smiles in a way that makes dimples dance on her plump cheeks. I decide I like her. On the third evening, Ted calls me into his small office off the bar.

'You're a good worker Lucy; no fuss, and you don't spend your time yapping to the customers. I like that. How would you feel about staying on here? The wage isn't great, only three quid a week, but you'll get room and board. What do you reckon?'

My sister, Maude, had worked briefly at the Albion. I have always wondered what it would be like to live independently, but still I worry about those things that I know Ma can't do, like chopping firewood, and so I point to a notepad and pen on his desk. He pushes it towards me.

> Will I be allowed to go home at the weekends?

'Not the weekends, that's our busiest time, but maybe on Mondays and Tuesdays. I reckon we could do without you then.'

I hold out my hand for Ted to shake, to seal the deal, then return to the kitchen sink with a purpose. At the end of the week, I hitch a ride on the mail van to Bairnsdale to have the stitches removed from my gum.

*

I have finished scrubbing the pots and am mopping the floor when I hear a ruckus coming from the front of the hotel. I am looking at Cook, my eyebrows raised in a query, when Ma bursts into the kitchen and wrenches the mop from my hands. My cheeks flame in anger.

'What do you think you're doing, girl? Leaving your ma to fend for herself. Your place is at home, not in a pub, working as a skivvy!'

She raises her hand to slap my face, then pulls back, remembering my jaw. She lowers her hand to her side.

'Get in the truck. Mr Carroll's taking us home.'

She turns on the solid heel of her lace-up shoes and heads out onto the road.

Frustration finds its way through my mouth in a scream. Ted comes running, expecting to find me injured, instead, he see tears streaming down my face. Cook tries to stop me, but I shrug her off, knowing I have no option but to follow my mother.

Ted runs after us, calling, 'Mrs Strobridge … I … please let's talk about this'. He catches up and confronts Ma.

'Your daughter is a hard worker, Mrs Strobridge and—you know what?—I think she likes working here. She's every bit as good as her sister was in the kitchen. You should be proud of her.'

'I will not have Lucy exposed to the drunks from the bar. Her place is in our home, with me. She needs to look after me, not your guests.'

She grabs my arm and hauls me towards Tom Carroll's truck, and I can see by the way he looks at me he is not pleased to be a part of this scene.

Back at the huts, I grab a heavy lump of wood and walk up and down the wall outside my mother's hut, bashing the slabs and howling like a wild animal. When I grow tired, I climb Dingo Ridge to sleep in my cave.

1951

I spend my days on Dingo Ridge wielding my axe, dropping the trees I had ringbarked five years before, then reducing them to fire-sized logs. I barrow each log down the hill to stack, ready for the winter fires, outside our two huts.

Preparation for winter includes renewing the layers of newspaper on the walls of Ma's hut to keep the winter chill from seeping through the gaps between the sheets of bark. A thick glue of flour and water runs down the wooden handle of the broad paintbrush onto my hands. I apply sheet after sheet from a pile of newspapers that I have saved for just this task. One sheet causes me to pause: a black-bordered rectangular box containing the words:

> *The Art Training Institute,*
> *Swanston Street, Melbourne,*
> *calls for interested parties*
> *to sit for the Entrance Certificate*
> *and Guarantee of a position as a student.*

I pull the tacky sheet of paper from the hessian wall and squat on my haunches, absorbing the information. I have always kept my drawings to myself, but I know they are good. I take the sheet of paper up to Dingo Ridge and crawl into my cave in the rock, not knowing whether I am too late to apply for a place—the paper is months old—but the thought of learning how to refine my art excites me to the core. I don't return to my hut to sleep that night. In my dreams, all my charcoal creatures crawl from their trunks surrounding me with warmth and encouragement.

The next day I run down the hill, straight into Ma's hut and fling the sheet of newspaper, stiff with dried glue, onto the kitchen table.

Ma reads the article, then screws it into a ball and throws it onto the fire.

'Don't be ridiculous! You're thirty-two, and you can't even draw.'

I ignore the invective—my drawings are my own private business—and jump on the notice before it can catch alight. Ma recognises the determination in my eyes and dares not defy it.

Grabbing a piece of charcoal from the fire, I draw a manna gum flower in all its fine detail on the pad Ma keeps for writing her grocery orders. She takes it over to the door and tilts it towards to daylight, studying it closely. She folds it in half and places it in her pocket as she turns to me.

'I can't see that you'll succeed, girl, but if you do, I'll pay for your course.'

*

Blizzards rage outside my two-roomed home, banking snow to the roof, filling the gap between it and the bark hut where Ma sleeps. Each morning I take a shovel and clear a path leading to the toilet platform on the rise above the huts, then remove the central plank and plant my feet firmly either side of the hole and bare my backside to the biting wind before emptying the bucket Ma insists on using during the night. Each afternoon I work on my drawings to submit to the Art Training Institute. It has taken a few weeks for my order of a sketch book to arrive via the Swifts Creek store. I now fill each large blank page with my finest creations.

Spring melts the snows as I finish drawing a wombat on the final page of the sketch book. There are no cattle to take to the mountain this year, Uncle Jeff has sold them all, but I escape to Dingo Ridge to set a line of rabbit traps, and the harvest is rich. I skin the rabbits while the dew is still on the grass and stretch them on the bow. The pelts I sell to the rabbiter weigh more that way, and my savings grow. I add them to the £3 Ted gave me for my work at the Albion Hotel.

I shoulder my bag of charcoal and ride into the ash forest. Nearly every smooth trunk bears my mark. Some have faded with time; some are so crisp, the animals leap from the trunks as if alive.

Ma is travelling to Melbourne this spring. The last time the Brothers visited to read their Bibles and collect her contributions, I listened through the wall as they strongly suggested that she should attend the Jehovah Witness Convention where, for three days, she can saturate her soul in sermons, forums and theatrical productions of Bible stories. They added that, if she brings her wayward daughter along too, they will baptise me with others, fully immersed in the waters of the Lord to cleanse my spirit.

When the Brothers collect Ma from her hut, she carries in her suitcase my sketchbook to hand-deliver to the Art Training Institute, along with my application to be accepted as a student.

*

Saturday by Saturday, I watch through the window in my front wall as Ma wheels the cane pram from Carroll's farm with the weekly groceries and mail. Each time, I intercept her and rifle through the newspapers and envelopes.

One day, a truck pulls up outside and a man gets out and opens the passenger door. To my surprise, Ma climbs out followed by a young lad, then the man and his son lift the loaded pram from the back of the truck. I have never seen them before. I wait for the truck to rattle off along Charlotte Spur Track, then emerge from behind a tree, stopping Ma so I can search for my longed-for envelope.

'That was Russ Boucher. He's just bought a farm down the track,' explains Ma. I'm not listening, my mind is focussed on just one thing.

'The kid's very quiet. Doesn't say much. His name's Chips. It seems a funny name for a kid.'

At the bottom of the pram lies a large brown envelope with 'Lucy Strobridge' in bold type, and the imprint of the Art Training Institute in the top left-hand corner. Hugging it to my chest, I disappear inside my hut. My fingers tremble as I tear open the flap. Carefully, I pull the prospectus from the envelope.

I have passed the entrance examination. With Honours. I am guaranteed a place as a student. Ma has no option now but to make good her promise.

The cover of the prospectus represents a world as far removed as possible from the one I inhabit. A heroic, almost god-like man wears a bright red Australian flag draped across his shoulders. One hand holds a sword high in line with the Southern Cross, the other rests on a shield of the Australian coat-of-arms. I turn the page …

> *This book is dedicated to all those, be they young or not-so-young, rich or not-so-rich, ambitious or merely Art-loving, who are looking for the key to the great career of ART.*

I have no idea if I can use my art as an escape from Ma, as the prospectus promises, but I allow my thoughts to escape the grip of my mother. It is a first step. I have wondered if others think I am any good, and my acceptance into the institute has proved that I am. I want to learn how to improve, to draw faces that don't scoff at my attempts. With a certain amount of pride, I take the book to show Ma.

'It looks a bit grand,' is her reply. I turn to the page that most excites me: a picture showing all the equipment that will be mine— as soon as Ma posts the cheque for my fees. Jars and tubes of paint, sable brushes, pencils, a drawing board, paper … equipment I have seen in magazines and dreamt of owning for so long.

'I can't see what good all this is going to do you, Lucy. You'll never get a job as an artist, no matter how much you practice. These people don't belong in our world and we don't belong in theirs.'

It takes Ma nearly twelve months to post off her cheque for £7, securing a place for me.

1952

The first lesson, together with a large box, arrives with summer. I cut the string then tear the brown paper from the box. I spread newspaper on the table in my living room and lay out the equipment. Taking out four sable brushes—from broad tip to pin-point fineness—I brush them on my cheek. They feel like feathers. I mount a sheet of clean white paper on the drawing board—two feet wide—and lean it against the wall at the back of the table.

One by one I unscrew seven small jars, each containing a vibrant colour. I admire their rich hues as the pungent smell fills my nostrils. I pour a small amount of earth-coloured paint from one of the jars into a mixing saucer and dip the tip of the broadest brush, then sweep it across the paper in the arc of a mountain. My mountain. Mount Delusion. Then another brush, another pot, and trees begin to grow up the mountainside. Blue from a tube produces the sky, across which float white clouds. Birds take flight. Wallabies graze. For the first time, my imaginative world holds colour. I stand in awe of what I have just created.

When the first sheet fills, I pin it to my wall, tack a second one on the board and continue to paint the animals I love. I ignore the pencils, set square and protractor—no doubt they will have their uses later—but for now I need to lose myself in this magical world of colour that has been granted to me.

By the end of the week, when my walls are papered with my artwork, I finally open the instruction book.

Lesson one.

I read of the correct posture for an artist, sitting or standing upright to ease muscle strain—but what good is that? I need to be up close, to see exactly what I am painting—then the section on lighting arrangements. This causes me to chuckle. How can I control the light that enters my hut when there is but one small window in the end wall which the sun never finds, and my kerosene lamp does little to change the situation?

I do, however, take more notice of the importance of proportion. While I usually draw objects as I see them, sometimes an animal's head does not fit comfortably on its body. I hold up a pencil in my left hand and, closing my right eye, move the pencil up and down the wall. It has never occurred to me before to use such a tool to check for proportion. Looking down my leg to my foot, I began to understand the principles of foreshortening.

The instruction book demands I complete sixty-four sketches, each addressing some aspect of painting, before I can progress to lesson two. Because the course focuses on commercial art, I need to reproduce clear, precise illustrations, a fact that suits me well. After all, I always try to render exact copies of my animals and trees.

For two weeks I barely step outside my hut, except to empty Ma's night bucket and set her fire. In the evening, I milk Pansy. The smell of turps and oil paint seeps into my pores. Twice a day, Ma cooks a meal which she leaves on my doorstep, taps on the rough-hewn door to let me know it is there. Often, she returns to find the bowl of stew congealed, untouched.

When I have completed all the set tasks, I bundle up my drawings, addressing them to the Art Training Institute, then walk to Carroll's farm. I hide behind a bush beside the driveway, waiting until Mr and Mrs Carroll leave their house to check on their cows, then slide in the front door and leave the parcel on their kitchen table for Mr Carroll to take to the post office at Swifts Creek.

A fortnight later my second instruction book arrives with a letter from my instructor, Walter Jardine.

> *Dear Miss Strobridge*
> *I am pleased to receive your sketches from lesson one. There is little doubt you possess great skill and have a future in the world of Commercial Art. You have executed all of these tasks to my complete satisfaction, although I notice you have included subjects that have not been required: wombats, lyrebirds and wallabies to name a few.*
> *While I admire your touch with the native wildlife, I suggest you limit further submissions to the tasks required.*
> *I look forward to a long and mutually pleasing association.*
> *Yours sincerely*
>
> *Walter Jardine*

I flick through lesson two but can find little to interest me. I skip through instructions on how to use the compass and protractor in order to draw cones, cylinders, prisms, pyramids, skeleton cubes and rings, and focus on the more demanding challenge of drawing furniture. I know exactly which piece of furniture I will draw.

Bursting into Ma's hut, I grab one of six chairs that sit, gathering soot from the fire, around the central dining table. Each has been hand carved by a man from Tambo with a lyrebird dancing across the top bar. I have found a way of following Mr Jardine's instructions while satisfying my own desires.

By the time lesson four arrives, Mr Jardine has stopped advising me to stick to the subjects. When I open the instruction book, I smile broadly. At last, they know what I want.

> *The intention is for the student to develop artistry by freely designing flowers and bush scenes for use on wallpapers and floor coverings.*

Instead of working on thirty-seven designs, as instructed, I carefully and intricately draw a hundred flowers, feathers and leaves on the ivory card provided, using five graded pencils—a far cry from lumps of charcoal on tree trunks.

Summer turns to autumn, winter knocks at my door, but I barely notice. I withdraw even more from the outside world, but my mind expands with new knowledge. Lesson by lesson, I try different techniques, making use of the specialist tools supplied by the Art Institute. I almost forgive Ma for forcing me to return from the Albion Hotel, although I still choose to ignore her; this is much more rewarding than scrubbing dishes.

The day arrives, as I know it must, when Ma insists I prepare the firewood for winter before the snows come. I take my axe and barrow and climb Dingo Ridge for the first time in five months. The axemen have long left the mountain and my charcoal sketches on the tree trunks have faded. Most have disappeared but I don't redraw them, instead, I hurry down to my hut with each load of firewood, eager to return to my artwork.

With the shortening days and the sun not reaching the valley floor, the light finally becomes too dim for me to continue my lessons and besides, I have grown bored with forming perfect letters, reproducing architectural perspectives and many other skills as instructed by Mr Jardine. The winter that follows is too bleak for me to escape into the mountains. I wrap up as warmly as I can and stay close to my hut; there is little to entertain me as the birds are either hiding as well or have moved on until warmth returns.

Every few weeks Mr Jardine writes enquiring why I have not completed my tasks. I don't bother to answer as there is nothing to say. Away from Ma's ears I sing the few songs I know and long for the sun's return so I can resume my lessons.

1953

I open the envelope from the Art Institute and read Mr Jardine's instructions for lesson thirteen—The Human Figure.

No fewer than 169 drawings of the human figure and its sections accompany these lessons and ensure complete mastery of a vital subject. I suggest you ask a friend to pose for these drawings.

I have no friends. Maud has moved onto a farm nearby, but she is busy with her own family and cows and I don't feel I can ask my sister to give up precious time to simply sit and be drawn. And Ma? Our relationship has deteriorated to basic actions: I empty her night bucket and supply firewood; Ma deposits my meal on my doorstep twice a day.

Each page shows different parts of the body from different angles. I do not possess a ball to hold in my left hand (as instructed), so I select a freshly laid egg and draw what I see. The result is pleasing. For the next few days I draw all the parts of my body that I can see, but when it comes to drawing a face, I have no idea how to proceed. I try sketching an eye from memory, but it lacks conviction. If only I could see my own eye—but there is nothing in my hut that I can use as a mirror, and Ma would never allow such an item in the house. She says to look upon your own reflection is to worship yourself and ignore Jehovah; only through studying the Bible can you see your true self. Of course I do not agree, but it is useless to try to argue with her.

I put down my pencil and pick up a mail-order catalogue from the bundle on the chair by my bed. Sandy often includes them with the weekly grocery order and the pictures of all manner of objects feed my dreams. Ma refuses to open the catalogues—they also are a temptation sent by the Devil; I consider them to be luxuries and would never place an order, but they remind me of the few days I spent working at the Albion.

I thumb through the pages of farm equipment, moleskin pants, cotton shirts, elastic-sided boots, kitchen utensils, then pause in the section on bathroom accessories. I have never taken any notice of mirrors before. Every size and shape, from cosmetic mirrors to full-length cheval mirrors in red cedar frames, there for the asking. One mirror, within a modest wooden frame, looks perfect for my purpose and doesn't cost too much. I carefully cut the picture from the catalogue and write across the image:

1 of these

I place the illustration in a brown paper bag along with a pound note from my savings, however I am unsure how to get my order to Sandy's store without Ma knowing.

The sound of a truck pulling up outside disturbs my thoughts. Through my window I see a man approach Ma's door with a box of groceries in his arms. I recognise him as Neil Fairweather who bought Uncle Jeff's farm last year. I creep into the space between the two huts to listen through the gaps in the slab wall.

'Tom Carroll's decided to give up his run into Swifts Creek, so I'll be doing your groceries and mail from now on Mrs Strobridge. I figured you'd like me to drop them in personally, seeing I drive right past,'

'That's very kind of you, Mr Fairweather. I'll put the kettle on. You will stay for a cuppa? Just put the box on the table there.'

Through a crack, I see him sit at the table and remove his hat. Ma begins chattering about this and that. I have forgotten how much my mother's harsh voice grates on me. I wait until Ma pours Mr Fairweather's cup of tea then slip out to his truck. I place the paper bag on the driver's seat where he can't help but see it, then return to my hut and my conundrum—but I can't block out Ma's conversation that rasps on for half an hour, leaving few gaps for her visitor to speak.

Finally, I snap. Grabbing a stout branch from beneath a tree, I walk around Ma's hut, bashing the wall, emitting blood-curdling guttural noises until Neil Fairweather collects his hat and runs to his truck, grinding his gears along Charlotte Spur Track to escape my racket.

*

A few weeks later I watch from behind my window as our new delivery man turns into Charlotte Spur Track then slows, looking towards the huts. He wheels in between two trees and edges his truck forward. He reaches into the tray-back and removes a rectangular parcel wrapped in corrugated cardboard and bound with rope, and looks towards my hut.

Ma shouts from her door, 'I'll put the kettle on, Mr Fairweather'.

'Thanks Mrs Strobridge. I'll just deliver this parcel to Lucy first.'

'What parcel?'

I can hear objection in Ma's voice.

'A mirror.'

I wait for the explosion.

'That can't be right. Lucy has no use for a mirror. You must be mistaken.'

He heads to my door and knocks.

'Hello Lucy, I've got a parcel for you, if you promise not to growl at me again.'

I sit very still at my table, holding my breath, waiting for him to leave the parcel and go.

'I'll just leave it here by your door.'

Neil returns to his vehicle and lifts a bundle of red-brown fur from the passenger seat. It looks like an animal, but it doesn't move. He walks to Ma's hut and I follow, curious. He hands the bundle to her.

'Mrs Fairweather wants me to give this to you. She reckons you need it more than she does.'

Ma unfolds a full-length fur coat and holds its softness to her face.

'Oh, I couldn't possibly accept this!'

'Why not? The missus never wears it now, and you must get pretty cold here. Keep it for when the snows come. You'll be surprised how warm it'll keep you.'

Ma refolds it and places it inside a wooden box she uses for storing her spare clothes, then turns to attend to the kettle pushing steam from its spout.

'Tell her thanks.'

I return to my parcel and cut the rope and remove the cardboard packaging. The timber frame feels smooth beneath the palm of my hand. I rest it on the table and lean it against the wall, then back away until, for the first time in my 35 years, I can see my entire body. The outline of my thighs through my cotton dress is strong, my shoulders are lean and square, my shoulder-length hair is the colour of straw, as Billy had always said. I move closer and see that my eyes are speckled green. I never knew that.

I sit on a chair looking directly at my reflection. This time my pencil is true to the image before me. I move closer and study my face with an artist's eye and my features transfer from the mirror to my pad, capturing my strong, angular jawbone and high cheekbones.

Each day I draw a different part of my body. On the second week, despite the sleet outside and the chill in the room, I remove my shirt and capture the firm lines of my shoulders; the soft curve of my breasts.

*

Ella removes her woollen gloves and engages the wheel of a can opener on the rim of a tin of Irish Stew. A puff of air hisses from the can as the small blade pierces the lid. She imagines it feels warm against her hands.

The relentless rain, freezing to the point of sleet, drums on the tin roof, forcing its way through pinholes left by rust, and drips through the bark that the tin is meant to protect. It plays out a rhythm as it plinks into strategically-placed iron buckets.

Ella worries about Lucy's obsession with her drawing, convinced that the Devil now inhabits her daughter's hut and has worked His way into her soul since the arrival of the mirror. It takes up precious time that should be spent tending the vegies in their little plot or trapping rabbits for the pot. She even has to remind Lucy to milk the cow and fetch firewood for the coming winter and stack it close by her door.

In the centre of the room, a fire flares as new twigs catch, causing Ella's shadow to dance on the walls of the old hut and fine wood ash begins to settle on the shoulders of her coat. Ella rotates the wings on the can opener slowly, for both it and her hands are stiff with cold and age. Briefly, the drumbeat on the roof and the crackle of the fire fall in time: chill and heat in unison.

Ella is uncomfortable in her fur coat, not because of the way it fits, but because Mrs Fairweather gave it to her to wear when the snow lies thick on the ground, and it isn't snowing. It seems indulgent to wear such a garment inside her home, and yet it is the only way, along with her woolly cap and gloves, of staying warm.

She bangs the bottom of the can with the palm of her hand and the stew slides reluctantly with a moist suck into an aluminium saucepan. She balances the pan on the inside edge of the rocks which define the limits of the firepit and, year by year, sink further into the earthen floor beneath the scraping blade of the ash shovel.

Robbed of the crimson firelight, her shadow stops dancing on the walls.

As the stew begins to bubble, Ella stirs it with a tablespoon, polished so often the silver coating has long disappeared, and tests the temperature of a cube of beef against her bottom lip. She knows Lucy will be angry if it is too hot or too cold, and she can already hear her moving about inside her hut, not ten feet from her own.

She ladles half the stew into a china plate and opens her door to cross the boggy ground between the two huts, aware that piercing green-speckled eyes are watching her every move through the crack of the partly opened door. She does not look up as she places the plate on the doorstep and raps twice before shuffling back to her own hut where she brushes the rain drops from her coat. Mother and daughter sit, each in her own hut, eating from the same tin of stew.

Late in the afternoon, Ella passes by Lucy's window on her way to retrieve the lunch plate and sees the work of the Devil himself—Lucy, stripped to the waist, looking at her own reflection in the mirror, cupping her breast as if feeling its weight. Her daughter bends her head and commences to draw. Enraged at witnessing such evil, Ella flings open Lucy's door and strikes her daughter across the face.

'Filthy girl! You will burn in hell for touching yourself!'

Lucy grabs her shirt and holds it to her chest, raising one hand to her burning cheek. Tears sting her eyes. She is powerless to explain.

Ella gathers the drawings scattered across the table, averting her eyes from the well-drawn nipple and curve of her daughter's body, which she has not seen since Lucy was a small child, and marches to her own hut to throw them on the fire.

'Let that be an end to this sinfulness,' she says as the sheets of card curl, darken and crumble to ash.

*

When the leaden skies are at their darkest, I pull on my warmest coat and ride Ginger to the top of Mount Delusion. I cannot remain in the hut beside Ma.

I miss the summers on the mountain with the cattle and quietly curse Uncle Jeff for selling out. Snow gently pats upon my bare head, soothing me. Ginger responds to the kick of my heels and gallops through the snow gums. The wind picks up and needles of ice sting my cheeks. Ginger's increasing speed does not frighten me and, anyway, I have no way of stopping him until he gallops to a standstill, panting and exhausted.

Reluctant to leave the mountain, despite the growing storm, I turn Ginger and head down the southern side, slackening his pace to enjoy the forest that surrounds me. As we drop in altitude, alpine ash begin to appear among the thinning snow gums; first one, then a couple. As their numbers grow, the snow gums hunch below the ash until they finally disappear. In their place, huge tree ferns appear at the feet of the forest giants. Birds become more vocal now there is a safe place for them to hide and play.

As always, the destruction caused by the loggers on these slopes angers and saddens me. Knowing they have left for the season, I follow their wheel tracks as they wind through gullies and ridges I haven't ridden for years—not since the days when I brought our cattle this way.

It is only when I am in thick ash and tree fern that I come across a structure altogether foreign to this place. Halfway down the mountainside, nestled in the protective fold of two ridges, stands a two-roomed hut. Its galvanised iron chimney faces the track, the weather boards are painted red-brown, and the timber door stands ajar.

I rein Ginger in and watch from behind a large trunk, barely breathing lest my presence should be discovered. Ginger flicks his ears, strained, just like mine, for the sounds of human activity, but there is no-one about. I dismount and approach a partly open door along the far side of the hut. I push the door and sidle inside. The dim interior smells much like my own hut—damp and smoky. Pinpoints of daylight shine through holes in the fireplace at the far end. There is just enough daylight through two windows, grown green with mould in this damp forest, to see that the walls are lined with newspaper. Firewood lies stacked in the fireplace, with tins of stew and Spam lined up across a mantelpiece. So, they even eat the same as I do. A guitar, much the worse for wear, leans in the corner near the fireplace.

I assume that this hut has been built by the loggers who spend the summers here cutting ash. I walk outside and look around. The forest grows right up to its walls, but beyond the distant gully, where once mountain spurs bristled with alpine forests, the slopes are now bare.

Surprised at the fury of the storm that followed me down the mountain, I tether Ginger in the lee of the hut and run inside—it might belong to the loggers, but I have every intention of taking advantage of its shelter. I light a fire and empty a tin of stew into a battered old saucepan. Looking for water, I go outside again and find a large pond contained by an earthen bank and fed by water bubbling from a spring. Beyond the dam, a tunnel lined with rusted galvanised iron zigzags its way into the hill. I follow the tunnel into a space, black as pitch. My gumboots squelch on the muddy floor. I feel something wriggle inside my boot. I hate leeches. This hole in the hillside makes my flesh crawl.

For two days the storm rages and I remain in the forestry hut. On the second day, I pick up the old guitar and brush my fingers across its rusty strings. I feel the vibrations through its back against my belly and feel joy. I stop the string with my finger on one of the metal strips across its neck and pluck the string again. The note changes. I try another spot on another string, and it changes again. I find I can play a tune by letting my fingers dance around it, and I pick out tunes I know. I sing and, with no-one to hear me, the words come out clear to my ears.

On the third day I feel my anger has ebbed enough to return to Ma. I try not to think of how my drawings curled in the fireplace as the flame caught the edges and raced to consume each sheet.

Back in my own hut, I am surprised to find my mirror still where I had left it leaning against the wall. Defiantly, I look at my face and promise that I will start again. Ma cannot stop me. This time, I will hide everything I do from her so she will never know.

1954

Each time Neil Fairweather drives in with the mail, I expect my next lesson to arrive. Weeks turn to months and still no parcel arrives from the Art Institute. I write a note that I leave with my lunch plate.

Where are my lessons?

My evening meal arrives with a note from Ma.

I cannot keep paying for the work of the Devil. I have cancelled your classes.

This time, hatred and anger totally consume me. I collect my waddy from outside my front door and stride around Ma's hut, banging the walls with all my strength, screaming with all my might, afraid to enter my mother's hut, knowing without a shadow of doubt that I will kill her if I come within striking distance. *And I do not care!*

*

Ella knows utter terror as she crouches beneath the kitchen table, listening to her daughter's rage increase with each circuit of the hut. She waits until Lucy is at the far corner then runs through the door and continues, as fast as her aging legs can carry her, towards Carroll's farm.

*

My cheeks are wet with tears as I lie on my bed, spent by the ferocity of my emotions. The room spins as my mother's words bounce off the walls. The lessons have formed the core of my existence for the past eighteen months and she has cancelled them. Sobs take the place of the tears and my body shakes uncontrollably. Eventually I pull my blankets over my shivering legs and collapse in an exhausted haze as the wombat shuffles out on his nightly patrol.

I wake to cold metal clamping my wrists behind my back. Memory and fear come flooding in as I spin my head and see the shiny buttons of the police sergeant's uniform. He pulls me to my feet. I have no strength left to fight as he drags me towards his car where the doctor waits.

This time, Ma's face bears no trace of remorse when the policeman drives me to Bairnsdale General Hospital.

*

I fix my eyes on the caged light bulb directly overhead—the same light that had glared relentlessly over me fourteen years before. Unfamiliar noises once again penetrate the brick walls, but the woman in the next bed does not count to twenty. I wonder what has become of her. Did she die? Did anybody care? I wriggle my fingers against my sides bound in a straightjacket and wish I could die. I doubt Ma would care.

I have never known such anger, such frustration. I no longer have control over my emotions and it truly frightens me. My artwork had been a lifeline to the world beyond the cold damp valley on the side of Mount Delusion, and my mother's constant criticism had been replaced by words of encouragement from Mr Jardine who, I believe, genuinely thinks I have talent. I had even begun to think that, just maybe, I could find employment when I had learnt all there is to learn. Now, this has all been ripped from me. By my mother.

Does anyone know I'm here? Last time, Mr Carroll had written to my father. He had cared and come to rescue me. Who is there to speak for me this time?

*

Neil Fairweather doesn't particularly like visiting Ella Strobridge. He finds her constant chatter irritating but he feels obliged to sit and sip tea with her as he doubts she receives many visitors, apart from the Jehovah Witness Brothers. He usually senses, rather than sees, Lucy during his visits—small things, like the snap of a twig outside followed by a low growling if he stays too long—but he has not felt her presence for over a month.

'How is Lucy?' he asks Ella, hoping to discover the young woman's whereabouts.

'Not here. She's not well. I sent her to hospital.'

'Oh, I am sorry to hear that. Is there anything I can do?'

'She's better off where she is. We both are.'

Obviously, Ella has no intention of providing further information. He bids her farewell and drives to Swifts Creek to deliver the orders to Sandy, but he can't quell his concern for Lucy.

'You don't know anything about what's going on at the Strobridges, do you Sandy?'

'Only that the old bat has sent the lass off to the loony bin again. Apparently Lucy went all psycho and had to be restrained. The sarge took her off in his car.'

'But surely Lucy isn't? Mad, that is?'

'No, I reckon it's old Ella who's really mad, but Lucy threatened her, and it was either put her in hospital or charge her with assault.'

Neil hands over his collection of orders and walks across the road to the doctor's house. Mrs Freeman answers the door and shows Neil into the waiting room.

Doctor Freeman's large frame has shrunk over the years, as has his head of black straight hair. He walks with a stoop, causing his jacket to assume the look of having been donned carelessly. This year, he turns 70, time to hand over the care of the people of the district to a younger man. He beckons Neil into his room.

'What can I do for you Neil? Are you feeling poorly?'

'No, it's not me I want to talk about Doc, it's Lucy Strobridge. Now, I know it's probably none of my business, but it bothers me that her mother can have her sent away and no-one seems to question it.'

Doctor Freeman pushes his chair away from his desk and folds his hands over his ample stomach.

'It's not an easy situation, Neil. I've been looking after them since young Billy died back in '36, and I've never known Lucy to utter one word since then. As far as I can tell, there's nothing physically stopping her, Lucy just doesn't seem to talk. I know this causes communication problems between Lucy and her mum—although they seem to have worked out their own ways. Mostly, Lucy writes down anything she wants to say. Lucy has got a temper on her, I'm afraid to say, and she frightens the bejesus out of Ella.

That's why I had her committed last time, and that's why they took her away this time.'

'Any idea what started it?'

'I think it had something to do with Ella refusing to continue paying for Lucy's art lessons.'

'I've noticed that the parcels have stopped coming from Melbourne. If that's so, it's a real shame. I'm sure they meant a lot to Lucy. Is there nothing we can do?'

'I'm heading down to Bairnsdale next Monday, maybe we could look in on her, if you'd like to come.'

'I certainly would. Thanks Doc.'

'Meet me here at eight.'

*

The hospital superintendent unties my hands to allow me to write on the piece of paper on his table. Before him is my file written by his predecessor.

'Now Lucy, I would like to know why you attacked your mother.'

I grab the paper and scribble in bold writing, so that he is in no doubt how I feel:

I didn't

He turns the paper so he can read it. I grab it from him and add to it:

I just hit her walls

'She was afraid you would harm her.'

But I didn't

'I need to know you are not a threat,' he says. 'For now, we will leave you out of the jacket. If you can prove to me that you have control of your anger for the next month, we shall reassess you. Do you understand?'

Of course I do, I'm not an idiot. But the words remain in my head and I nod, allowing the wardsman to escort me to my bed.

Day after day I lie on my side and stare at the wall, afraid to think in case my anger rises again. I obey all orders, take part in activities, but I jump, startled, whenever the beep of a car horn penetrates the brick walls.

Four weeks later I am again summoned to the super-intendent's office where, to my shock, I find Doctor Freeman and Neil Fairweather seated at the desk. The sight of the doctor stirs terror in the pit of my stomach. They rise as I enter the room and the superintendent points to a vacant chair. I turn to run but am blocked by a burly wardsman. If I try to escape, this grim hospital will be my home for the rest of my life. I turn to face my audience.

'Please take a seat Lucy. It appears you have people who care about you. Mr Fairweather and Doctor Freeman have assured me they will take responsibility for your wellbeing, should I see fit to release you.'

I look at the two men, puzzled as to why they, particularly the doctor, would do this for me.

'Are you happy to return to Brookville?'

How can I be happy, living alone with my mother. She stops me whenever I find something I enjoy.

I nod. The alternative—to stay in the hospital—is too horrible to contemplate.

'Doctor Freeman has recommended that you receive the disability pension of seven pounds per fortnight. This means you will not need to rely on your mother for your every want and it will give you a degree of independence, should you wish. Please sign these forms where I have placed a cross.'

*

I curl into the corner of the back seat as these two men drive me to Swifts Creek, unsure how my life will unfold. As we pull into Sandy's store a stocky man, trailing a young boy, walks out of the front door and raises his hat to me. I am sure he is the man who gave Ma and her pram a lift a couple of years ago.

'We can take Lucy home, no problems, I'm heading that way now,' he says to Sandy. He waves me over to his truck and opens the door.

'There you go Lucy. Young Chips can squeeze in between us.'

The lad springs into the middle of the bench seat and I climb up beside him. Mr Boucher chatters about this and that as he crashes through the gears, but Chips just stares at me the whole way home.

Ma stands at her doorway, hands on hips, as I clamber down from the cab. I cannot look at her. From this day on, I will have nothing more to do with my mother.

I return to the familiar sounds of lyrebirds, cockatoos and the scrape of the wombat's fur on the side of my hut; the comfort of Pansy's full udder as milk squirts into the galvanised iron bucket; daily chores, and silence between myself and Ma. When the loggers return to their coupe, I imagine them gathering at night by the fire in their hut on the slopes of Mount Delusion, playing the guitar.

*

Days come and go, then weeks, then months, without a word spoken between Lucy and Ella. Each morning Lucy empties Ella's night bucket. Twice a day, Ella places a plate on Lucy's step, raps on the door, then retreats to her tumble-down hut to eat alone and spend her day in prayer and readings from her Bible, always in search of a passage to justify her actions and explain her daughter's.

The Brothers visit regularly to offer solace and collect her contributions. They always ask if Lucy has yet seen the Light. Each time, Ella feels profound failure in admitting that her daughter is a lost cause. She does not mention to the Brothers the visits from the Anglican minister, Fred Wandmaker, who also drinks tea from her china cups and offers solace.

Once a fortnight, when Neil Fairweather delivers the mail, he leaves an envelope on his driver's seat, which contains Lucy's pension cheque, a pen, and seven pounds from the previous fortnight. Lucy signs the back of the cheque and replaces it in the envelope, then collects the money which she hides in a shoe box in the bottom drawer of her dresser.

*

It is early morning as I take down the mirror from behind my table and gather my paints and pencils into my saddlebag. My heart is numb; my spirit broken. I know I will never draw again.

I ride Ginger to the middle of the forest that once bore my sketches on their smooth bark and dig a hole beneath the largest tree and bury my paints, my brushes, my dreams. It feels much the same as when they buried Billy. A gentle rain filters through the leaves; tiny drops cling to my hair. My cheeks are wet with rain and tears.

Mounting Ginger, I dig my heels into his sides but I make no attempt to guide him for I have no idea where I want to go. Ginger ambles westward, onto Mount Delusion, then follows the mountain track that leads to Grandma's house. I recognise where Ginger is taking me and feel the ghost of Billy's arms wrap around my waist. After all these years.

When we reach Wentworth River, instead of turning south to the old farm, I steer Ginger north and follow the river. I do not want to stand where Grandma's house had been. I prefer to remember the old tree house as it was when Billy and I last visited to sit by the fire and share our ghost stories.

Mountains rise high on either side as I ride through the wattles beside the narrow river, grateful for Ginger's surefootedness on the rocky path. Gradually, above the singing of the birds, I become aware of a different sound, like water tumbling onto rocks.

The trees grow closer together and I can no longer ride between them. I dismount and tie Ginger to a trunk and proceed on foot. Wombat and wallaby tracks follow the river as it disappears into a void to crash onto a shelf far below. I scramble down the tracks, grabbing ferns, roots and grasses as I half slide onto the ledge. The sound of falling water fills my senses.

I edge around a ledge on the sheer side of the hill, still following the animal tracks, then stare down to where the river disappears into a dim mist. The trees change to rainforest, dripping onto the ferns growing out of every crack in the rocks. Mosses cling to ancient trunks that never dry. Down I slide, mostly on my behind, until I reach the floor of the ravine. Ferns, still stiff with morning frost, glisten on huge rocks.

I settle on one of the rocks and watch as the sun gradually finds its way into the ravine, playing with the spray, creating haloes of light and rainbows that fill my world and my heart. Leaves and ferns catch the mist and turn it into a wonderland of sparkles. I have never seen a more beautiful place.

The river continues through the narrow gorge, slowing as it reaches a bend, spreading into a pool where little fish swim. It is too cold to swim this time, but now I know of this secret world, I will return. For now, I sit hugging my knees, breathing in the cool mist and breathing out the evilness of the hospital ward with its strict matron and straitjacket. I shudder at the memory. I will never go back, I promise myself and the river. I will never put myself in that position again. It was Ma's fault. I will have nothing more to do with her, then they cannot say I threatened her. As far as I'm concerned, she is dead to me.

This thought causes pain, and I feel very alone.

A wombat waddles around the corner following its track and pauses, one foot raised, when it sees me. It slowly turns its head as if to return the way it came, then changes its mind and walks past my leg, so close I can feel its body warmth. I sit very still, letting it pass at its own pace.

Hours later, I climb out of the ravine into a world that seems fresh and alive. The mists have done their job, renewing my spirit, reminding me that what I love most—the animals, the trees—are still here for me. I mount Ginger and head along the river to the track leading to the forestry hut. The loggers aren't on the mountain and I feel the need to play the guitar once more.

I approach the hut cautiously, but the way is clear. The guitar lies across a chair by the fireplace. I gather sticks from outside and build a fire to warm my hands, then pick up the instrument and strum my thumb across the strings, wondering if music could fill the hole left by my drawings. As day turns to night, I light the stub of a candle I find in a bottle on the table and open a tin of Spam left by the loggers. I feed the fire and continue singing as I strum the guitar, making up new words to fit the tunes I learnt at school as a child.

As the fire settles to red glowing coals, I pull a blanket from one of the stretchers in the other room and curl up on the splintery floorboards before the fire, dreaming of rainbows in the mist.

1960

I haven't seen my sister Maude for a few years. Whenever she visits Ma, I disappear onto Dingo Ridge. It's not that I don't wish to see her; it's just that I have nothing to do with my mother's world.

One day I don't hear her arrive when there is a gentle tap on my door. I say nothing, then the door slowly opens and my nephew, Raymond, enters. The lad is now as tall as me. His features are maturing and there is an unmistakable likeness in our faces.

'Gidday Aunty Lucy. Mum and Ma talk about boring things and I want to walk in the bush. I thought you might like to come too.'

He picks up my axe and walks out towards Dingo Ridge. He strides up the slope and I follow, puffing a little in an effort to keep up with my young, strong nephew. We reach a clearing where I have dropped a number of logs and he begins to chop them into manageable lengths while I sit on a fallen tree and watch, appreciating his wordless companionship. With two logs separated from the trunk, he hands me the axe and lifts one length to each shoulder with seemingly little effort, and heads down the hill to add them to the rest of the wood pile.

'I'm playing a game of footy next Saturday. I wondered if you'd like to come and watch.'

I nod acceptance and a grin spreads across his face.

'Would you really come? Oh, that is great! We'll pick you up on the way.'

I travel to the football ground in the back of their car, reliving bad memories of men in police uniform, but I grip the door handle and keep my nerve. For Raymond.

When we arrive at the ground I am dismayed to see so many people gathered, laughing, discussing their own days playing football. I sit on a weathered bench at the end, far away from the enthusiastic parents running along the sideline, shouting at their sons. I am unable to follow what is going on, but Raymond grabs the ball and runs the full length of the oval and everyone cheers. I feel proud.

At the end of the match, he takes me to a stall where they sell hot dogs and lemonade. I have never tasted a hot dog before. Tomato sauce dribbles down my chin and the front of my dress. We laugh as he takes a paper serviette and cleans it up.

He is growing into a fine young man and I like him. I look forward to his visits when we can walk in the bush together.

1964

'Do you smell smoke?' Arty straightens up, wiping sweat from the back of his neck with his handkerchief, scanning the forest to the south. The forest is so dry it crackles. It reminds him of the summer of '39, and he fears another fire season.

'Yeah, now that you mention it, I do,' replies Bob.

But they can't see any fire and they return to work on their particular giant.

Arty wonders how much longer he will be able to carry on logging. Approaching fifty, he is the oldest in the camp, a fact that is beginning to show as he leaps up onto the springboards embedded in the trunks. Twenty years ago, he had been first up the trunk, now his knees stiffen and once this season he missed his footing. In this business, a slip means death. By rights he should not still be working the forest, but he can't imagine living any other life. The rest of the crew has moved further up the mountain to another coupe. Bob and Arty will follow when they have finished.

The tree crashes to earth, just where they aim, and they begin stripping its branches. Arty pauses again and hears the unmistakable crackle of a fire racing through undergrowth.

'I can definitely hear it now! I don't think it's crowned yet.'

Fire always burns uphill. They have no option but to head for the dugout, a mile down the mountain, towards the fire, hoping it hasn't reached that far.

*

January arrives so dry that the canopy thins, allowing me to see much further into the valleys. The litter beneath my feet, normally moist, crunches as I walk through the forest. One morning I wake to the acrid smell of smoke and assume it is coming from the loggers' camp. When I take Ma's bucket to the platform on the rise I cannot make out the individual trees on Dingo Ridge. My whole valley wears a hazy blanket. This is no small loggers' campfire!

I saddle Ginger and gallop to the top of Mount Delusion to try to see which direction the heart of the fire lies, to work out if we are in danger. I can hear the fire from the southern slopes and take off down the loggers' tracks. An hour later I am confronted by a wall of flames racing through the dried bracken at the foot of the trees.

I know this slope well. The hut with the guitar is not far and, beside it, the dugout where I will find refuge. I dismount and turn Ginger free to find his own way home, then head for the dugout. The flames are reaching higher into the trees as they speed up the side of the mountain, exploding the oil-filled leaves, and I try to outrun them, hoping I will have the refuge to myself.

I stumble into a clearing made by the two axemen just as they are making for the dugout beside their camp. I follow the men through the zigzag iron tunnel into the blackness of the hole. One of the men lights a kerosene lantern, then stares in amazement as I appear in the flickering light.

'Bloody hell, where did you come from?'

I look around the ten-foot-square space, shored up against the earth by logs as thick as the men who cut them—walls and roof.

Horizontal logs form benches ready for a long wait. A forty-four gallon drum filled with water stands beside the entrance.

'Don't worry about that now,' says the other man, 'here, grab this'.

He dips a blanket into the drum to wet it thoroughly and throws it to me, pointing to a pole suspended above the doorway.

'Hang it over that.'

They each grab a grey woollen blanket which they saturate and drape over their shoulders, shouting at me to do the same.

The roar of the approaching fire swallows any further talk. I hunker down with the men to await the fire's passing and study their craggy faces caught in the glow of the lantern.

As my eyes adjust to the gloom, I see beards of moss growing on the walls, following the path of moisture seeping between the logs and trickling to the ground. It has formed puddles of mud that ooze between my bare toes. The mildewy smell of dampness fills my nostrils.

We know when the fire front comes. The entrance tunnel cannot stop the tremendous heat surging into the dugout. The men bucket water onto the blanket across the opening. It sizzles. One pours another bucket of water over my head and shoulders, yelling to stand against the back wall. Inside my cocoon of wet, musty wool, I listen for the cry of the animals that can't outrun this inferno, and of the alpine ash that will never recover.

The roar passes quickly with the fire. I pull the blanket from my head, feeling the wriggling of leeches on my legs. There is no sense pulling them off, they will only reattach and continue their feeding.

In the stillness that follows the firestorm, I become aware of the men staring at me, waiting, I think, for an explanation.

'I'm Arty and this is Bob,' says the older of the two men. 'You live down in those little huts with your mother, don't you?'

I nod.

'We seen you tripping about like a fairy.'

I thought my dancing in the forest had gone unseen.

'Don't talk much, do you?'

I shake my head as I rise to leave the dugout. I stop at the doorway and, turning, smile my thanks to the men. I emerge into a scene of horrible blackness. Smoke streams from still-burning trunks and the soil is the same burnt colour. Even with my toughened feet, I know I won't be able to cross the scorched earth. I return to the dugout.

'Thought you'd be back,' Bob grins. I point to one of the blankets and he hands it to me. I tear two strips from the end and bind each foot, then saturate them before stepping outside again. By a miracle, and the buffer of the dam full of water, the fire has wheeled away from the forestry hut. I think of the guitar and smile that it, too, has survived.

The track leading down the mountain to my hut stands out stark against the black landscape. At least, here, the bare ground is not burnt, but I curse the fact that I had not stopped to pull on my rubber boots as I leapt onto Ginger this morning. Once I am sure the ground ahead has cooled, I unstrap the pieces of blanket from my feet and begin the trek down the mountain to home.

For as far as I can see, the countryside is black. I cannot hear a bird, nor see any wallabies. With each corner I turn, I fear I will find the charred remains of Ginger. I cannot bring myself to think about what I will find at my hut.

As I approach the turnoff to Dingo Ridge track, black turns to green. The fire has not penetrated the moist gullies that surround my home. I scramble down the hill between the peppermint gums, past the forest I have ringbarked. The trunks stand, in their starkness, waiting to serve Ma's cooking fires.

Ginger lifts his head from grazing as I approach the hut and snorts a welcome. I stroke his soft ears and Ginger muzzles my neck. Ma comes out of her door, wooden prop in her hand, the task of boiling the clothes in the copper forgotten with my return.

'Ah Lucy girl, I truly thought you were dead. Ginger came back, alone. What else was I supposed to think?'

She returns to prod the sheets in the copper. I close the door on my hut and sit on my bed, reflecting on the day that has just passed. All my life I have avoided the loggers who I took to be monsters, but they were kind to me, and I do not know much kindness. I wonder which of them owns the guitar and if I will hear it make music one day.

1966

Spring has arrived on Mount Delusion and with it comes fresh shoots of snow grass. Ginger snorts gently as he steps through the new grass. My boots hang loose in the stirrups; we are not in a hurry to go anywhere. I shift my weight in the saddle, turning to watch a flock of yellow-tailed black cockatoos as they pass overhead. The breeze freshens, and I know it will soon be time to turn homeward, or find a place to shelter for the night. Even in spring, the nights are cold.

We pass a tangle of dead branches fallen from a gnarled old tree, and I make a mental note of their position. They may be handy to feed a fire should I decide to remain on the mountain. I like the idea. It has been too long since I stayed out in my shelters scattered across the landscape. Without any connection to Ma, I no longer feel the need to escape.

The daylight turns golden and shadows lengthen. Ginger snorts again, only this time, I notice a gurgling sound coming from his nostrils. An uneasy feeling settles in the pit of my stomach. Ginger is my constant companion. I tell him my secrets as we ride the mountains together. He has carried Billy's weight on his broad back; flown through the snow gums as we whooped in delight. Only once has he thrown me, and I did not blame him as I was showing off to Billy.

My feet suddenly don't hang so loose in the stirrups, but brace. For what, I don't know.

The sun finally dips below the horizon, taking the long shadows of the snow gums with it as wallabies emerge and begin to graze on the fresh new grass shoots. I finally need to make the decision whether to turn or stay. Night is close and cockatoos settle in a tree far below in the valley.

Then I notice a wheezing sound coming from Ginger and I know we must stay. I cannot ask him to ride down the mountain in the dark. I lean forward and fondle his ears. 'It's okay old fella, we can camp here tonight.'

I turn Ginger and retrace his steps to the fallen branches. His head hangs low and he doesn't respond as I gently push my heels into his flanks, spurring him on. He stops and I feel a quivering beneath my calves. The poor animal is gasping for breath. I dismount and remove the saddle from his back, hoping to ease his breathing, but he snorts again and I notice his eyes do not focus on me but stare blankly at the grass at my feet. He is old now, I know that, but it has never occurred to me that there will be a life without him.

I stroke his muzzle and whisper into his ear. It flicks beneath my warm breath. His knees buckle and he drops to the ground, his legs bent beneath his body. He wriggles them free and lies on his side. I hold his dear, dear head in my lap and sing gently to him until the night closes in.

I gather the fallen branches and light a fire to warm us both and lean against his distended stomach to gain a little warmth and give comfort to my mate. When I wake in the morning, the warmth has left the fire and his body. My grief is overpowering.

Crows circle, and I know dingoes will be waiting nearby. I feed the fire and stay by his side for two days, unsure what to do.

I cannot bear the thought of Ginger ending his days as food for wild animals. With his life gone, I collect as many fallen branches as I can find and heap them over his rigid, bloated body, creating an almighty bonfire. I hide my saddle in the hollow of a tree trunk and wait till his story is ended.

1970

I have grown used to wandering the bush and mountains on foot, mostly aimlessly. I never did retrieve my saddle. There is no use; I will never own another horse. At times I wonder why I exist. I serve no purpose. I give nothing to anyone and I receive nothing in return. Nothing ever changes here: Neil still delivers our groceries; occasionally, Maud visits Ma and Raymond and I walk through the bush; I plant vegies for our pot and collect eggs from the chooks – although that is one thing that has changed; someone has given us six ducks and I have made a cage to keep them safe from dingoes and foxes. Ma still cooks my meals and I still eat them. I still collect her night bucket, but sometimes it is empty and I don't know what this means. Is she ill?

Walking to Wentworth Falls takes a lot longer, and so I have made a lean-to near Grandma's old farmhouse where I stay. I wonder what Ma does with the contents of her night bucket when I am away.

This morning I rise with an urge to play the guitar again. It hasn't crossed my mind since Ginger died four years ago. It takes time to recover from grief. I set out while the frost is thick on the ground to walk the mountain. My backpack contains enough food for a few days as I intend staying a while. The climb seems much steeper than it did when I rode Ginger, but the once-dead forest now wears a coat of soft green where new saplings grow. Life does renew.

I approach the forestry hut cautiously even though I haven't heard the loggers on the mountain for a few weeks. I wait, hidden in the ferns, but there is no-one. Inside, I set my pack on the table and reach for the guitar, but it is not there. I search everywhere, pulling firewood from the box, behind chairs, tables, beneath stretchers, even under a pile of blankets.

I run to the dugout; of course, it will be there waiting to keep them company in case of a fire. It is not. I can't stem the flow of tears as I set a fire and warm my stew and sing songs, but my voice is flat and tuneless without the guitar to accompany it. Few things in life give me pleasure, and they are all taken from me. I remain in the forestry hut for only one night.

1971

Matthew Tulloch takes charge of the Swifts Creek Presbyterian church with every intention of serving each of his parishioners, no matter where they live. His predecessor issues him with a list of the outlying farms, giving him a rundown on each person.

'You might want to give the Strobridge farm a wide berth,' says Fred. 'Old Mrs Stroie is okay. She always makes a cup of tea and can talk the leg off an iron pot, but the daughter, Lucy, is a strange one. I've never been able to sit down and have a conversation with her. She is always running away up the hill, or stays in her own hut.'

'Her own hut? Doesn't she live with her mother?'

'Not on your Nellie! They had a falling out twenty-odd years ago and haven't spoken since, as far as I know. If I stay too long, Lucy kicks up an almighty racket and I have no choice but to leave.'

'Well,' says Matthew, 'we'll see about that. I find that a good listening ear goes a long way with troubled people'.

Fred smiles to himself.

'What if I take you around to introduce you? I would like to say goodbye to the old girl anyway.'

The two men part, agreeing to meet the following Saturday for a drive out to Brookville.

Ella greets the two ministers when they arrive, inviting them in to sit at her dining table while she boils the kettle and arranges three cups and saucers around the china teapot. She plays the perfect hostess, pouring each cup of tea through a silver tea strainer, ending with a flourish, even cocking her little finger as she sips from her cup. Matthew can't help thinking how incongruous this all is in such a primitive setting. Conversation continues as the sun throws lengthening shadows.

Suddenly, the serenity of the afternoon tea party is shattered by a loud bang on the wall. Matthew jumps out of his seat expecting the roof to collapse. Fred and Ella smile knowingly.

'This is usually my signal to depart,' Fred explains to Matthew as the banging grows louder and more rapid.

*

I have no time for visitors. They disturb my peace. Whenever the minister visits, Ma becomes very noisy, so I bang the walls of her hut with my waddy to make him leave. Today, he brings a new minister with him. I cannot allow this. I make more noise than usual with my banging and, for good measure, I throw in some growling noises. But he takes his time, finishing his cup of tea before walking to his car.

*

When Matthew Tulloch next visits Ella, she is full of apologies for her wayward daughter. Lucy has been away from her hut for a few days, so Ella feels more at ease, but even so, Matthew notices how sallow her complexion is.

'How are you feeling, Mrs Strobridge?'

Ella wants to tell him she has discovered a large lump in her breast, but how can she tell this to a man? Instead, she explains how she is constantly short of breath and how she no longer has the energy to do small things.

'If you would like, I can take you to see the doctor. It will be no bother.'

Lucy returns home from Wentworth Falls to see the minister's car disappearing down the road with her mother in the passenger seat.

1972

The fine seed heads drift before a faint breeze. All is so quiet, I can hear the tiny seeds rattle inside the pods. My gumboots leave deep impressions in the damp earth as I step from my door. I imagine I hear a faint whimper, but the breeze stiffens and the leaves begin to rustle, drowning the sound. Ma's night bucket stands by her door as it does every morning. The lovely golden light of early morning begins to lose is glow as the sun climbs higher. The breeze dies and I am sure I hear a whimper again, coming from Ma's open window. The breeze drops and the seed heads cease their movement.

I know I am stronger than most women, due, I guess, to walking miles over the hills and mountains. I think I am around fifty-three, but age means nothing to me as birthdays have never been celebrated in our home—it is against the will of Jehovah—and so, without the yearly ticking-off of calendar events, I have only a vague notion of my age. Life is something to endure until death takes its place. Day-to-day living is all that matters—and things like comfortable clothing. My gumboots, the only appropriate footwear for where I live, have become an extension of my legs. These days, I never step outside without them. My tough soles have become soft.

I stoop to pick up Ma's bucket. It is empty. The breeze springs into action again, waving the limbs of the manna gums, dappling what little sunlight filters through. A distant rumbling grows nearer. At first I cannot place the sound, then I hear the crunch of gears as a logging truck approaches the corner. I feel that my space is being invaded as the truck rolls into view then passes on its way up Mount Delusion.

Leaving the empty bucket, I climb the hill to the toilet platform. I squat over the hole, looking back at the two huts. Instead of the usual morning plume of smoke from Ma's chimney, I notice a thin spiral from yesterday's fire. Ma is such a creature of habit. By now, the kettle should be boiling for her first cuppa.

I creep to the wall, listening for sounds of movement. All I hear is rasping breathing, and that whimpering. I put an eye to a crack and see Ma sitting on a chair, leaning on the table. I pace backwards and forwards. I have not entered my mother's home for twenty years but now it seems I have no choice. As the whimpering turns to a gurgle, I push open the door and step into the gloom that is blackened by ancient smoke.

I inch my way to Ma's side, but she does not move. I stand behind her and pull her into a sitting position, but she stoops to the right and would have fallen had I not wrapped my arms around her and laid her back on the table. Fear and panic now grip me. I need help. The only person I can think of, close at hand, is Neil Fairweather. Leaving Ma lying on the table, I run along the track, following the wheel ruts made by Neil's truck.

The last time I came to this farm, Uncle Jeff still owned it, now the green Austin tray truck that delivers our weekly groceries is parked out front. I bang on the front door with my fists, but no-one answers. I hasten around to the back of the house to find Neil gathering eggs from the chook yard. I grab him by the arm, scattering eggs and chooks, and drag him to his truck, pointing back up the track. When we arrive at Ma's hut I wait for Neil to enter.

'Oh God! You poor dear! We'd better get you some help.'

He comes to the door and summons me.

'You'll need to give me a hand here Lucy. It looks like your mum's had a stroke. She's conscious, but can't move. We need to get an ambulance. You stay with her; I'll go home and ring Swifts Creek. I'll be as quick as I can.'

I push past him to Ma. I stroke her hair away from her face.

When the ambulance turns off the track into our yard, I slip out of Ma's hut and watch from behind my own window. Seeing men in uniform alighting from motor vehicles reminds me of the horror of being taken to Bairnsdale Hospital, and these men have arrived to take my mother to the same place—only for her, it will be the emergency entrance, not the ward at the rear with a cage around the electric lights.

*

I have never lived in my hut without the presence of another human close by. I hadn't realised how I draw comfort from the certainty that Ma is only ten feet away and always provides my meals.

My own hut, with my bed, has a fire but nowhere to cook a meal or boil a billy, so during the day, I sit by the fire in Ma's old slab hut and prepare my own meals, waiting for news. The fireplace in the corner is piled high with grey ash. Life without Ma is strangely quiet.

Occasionally, Maud arrives with a pot of stew or a meat pie. She tells me Ma has left the hospital and is now living with her family where they can take care of her. She tells me Ma doesn't have long to live.

Each week, Neil stops by to collect my grocery order. I write a list and leave it, with my money, on the kitchen table. When I hear his truck pull up, I hide in my bedroom hut until he leaves the groceries and drives off along Charlotte Spur Track.

The day Maude tells me that Ma has died, I escape onto Dingo Ridge, convinced that my sister is lying. Ma can't die! I need her here, to cook my meals, see off unwelcome visitors; to pee in her bucket each night. I have no doubt that Maude is hiding our mother from me. Maude says they will bury Ma in the Omeo cemetery, beside our father. The Jehovah Witness Brothers are paying for her funeral. I refuse to go. It is a trick. Ma is not dead.

*

Month by month, the pile of ash in the corner of Ma's hut grows higher until it covers the stones that support the cooking pot and kettle. Clearing the ash has always been Ma's task, one that I was not aware needed doing. The morning is warm and humid as I collect my shovel from the lean-to outside my bedroom hut. A few weeks ago, I fashioned a wheelbarrow from offcuts of the boards that form my walls and a wheel from the cane pram Ma used to collect our weekly grocery order from Carroll's farm. It makes life much easier for me as I bring the logs down from Dingo Ridge to feed the fire. I wheel the barrow beside the firepit and begin shovelling the ash to wheel outside and dig into the new vegie garden I am preparing.

I am used to the sounds of my bush and my mountain. Occasionally, strangers pass by; sometimes a car pulls up and a walker ventures to my door. I know they are walkers by their gear: khaki shorts, sturdy boots, drink bottles dangling from their hips or binoculars from their necks. I hide behind a tree and growl low, like a wild animal, and they usually scurry to their car and drive off as I chuckle to myself.

This morning, I hear a different noise from high up on Dingo Ridge. I stop clearing the ash and collect my rifle—tucking the butt in my armpit; filling the pocket of my apron with bullets—and climb the slope behind my huts.

Thud, thud, the noise continues. Then silence. Then another thud, thud. I creep closer to the source with my rifle raised at the ready. Near the top of the ridge, where young peppermint gums grow between mature trees, a man walks across the slope, swinging his axe, knocking out saplings. Sweat stains his cloth hat and drips from his bushy eyebrows. I take aim and send off one shot, carefully aimed, inches from his dusty boots.

'Holy mother of God!'

The man stands, stunned, facing me—a woman in gumboots, cotton dress and striped apron, pulling back the bolt and loading another shell. I push the pin to cock the rifle ready for my next shot.

'I don't know what your beef is lady, but I'm just doing me job. Jennings have sent me up here to knock out the suckers.'

The dust kicks up again, this time between his feet.

'Shit, I'll say this, you're a crack shot.'

I reload.

'You want me to go?'

Silly question. What do you think? How dare you interfere with my forest.

The sucker basher takes off across the slope, clutching his axe handle, swearing over his shoulder at what, to him, is a mad woman with a gun.

I walk down the hill and return to my task, convinced I have delivered my message; convinced the man from the sawmill will not bother me again.

The scraping of my shovel across the hardened earth as I finally reach the bottom of the pile of ash masks the sound of a car pulling up by the side of the track. I rake through the fine powder that now fills my wheelbarrow, seeking lumps of charcoal to replace on the hearth to give life to my next fire.

I lift the handles of the barrow and wheel it outside. Right in front of me is the police sergeant. The barrow, released from my grip, tips sideways spilling its contents on the doorstep. A cloud of ash rises, covering the sergeant and me alike. I reach for my rifle leaning on the wall by the doorframe, then realise I have not reloaded it after my confrontation this morning. The sergeant wrests it from my grip.

'That's what I'm after, thankyou Lucy. I had a visit from Mr Hardy this afternoon. It seems you frightened the life out of him. You can't go around shooting at people willy-nilly, you know. Now, I don't want any trouble—nor does Mr Hardy, he was only doing his job, after all—so I'll take this rifle and that way, you won't be able to accidently kill anyone.'

As he turns to leave, then makes a dash for his car with the rifle, I chase him, wielding my waddy—now my only means of defence—screaming at the top of my lungs.

*

That evening I sit by the light of my fire shivering, despite the mildness of the air. Outside, I can hear the boobook calling to his mate—she returns his call after waiting a good while—and scraping beneath the floorboards of the wombat setting out on his nightly prowl. I pull on the cardigan that has been part of my world for so long, I had forgotten that Ma knitted it. It is the only thing she ever made for me.

Another sound reaches my ears, one that does not come from any natural causes I know. Something hard lands on the tin roof and bounces across the corrugations. My shivering increases. I light a candle in a large jam jar and sit, holding my breath, anxiously trying to identify the strange sound when it comes again, but this time there is more than one object rattling across the roof. The boobook calls again, as if trying to answer my query.

The cardigan sleeves, knitted with a rib and stiff with years of washing, scrape across my bare arms, raising more goose bumps on my skin. A strong breeze whistles through the cracks between the slabs and the candle flickers, making shadows wriggle across my walls. Quiet returns for a few minutes, then another whistle that I am sure is not caused by the wind or any bird, rises eerily from the front of my hut. I have never felt so vulnerable, except perhaps when I lay in the narrow bed with my hands and arms bound in the straightjacket.

More objects bounce across my roof—thump, thump, thump. A light flashes through the window, sweeping across the wall, then abruptly disappears. Again, the eerie whistle, but this time, it is accompanied by a voice, calling, teasing me: 'Oh Mad Lucy, we are ghosts come to scare you!'

It is just kids! Suddenly, embarrassed at feeling so scared, I charge out of my door, waddy in hand, and scream at them, flogging the ground, creating my own version of noise to scare the living daylights out of *them*.

By the light of a nearly full moon I see two boys jump onto their pushbikes and ride down the track, driving their pedals as fast as their skinny legs can move. I return to my fire, my candle, and remove the cardigan; it now seems too hot.

*

I still expect Ma to return. Convinced Maud is hiding her, I freeze my sister out of my life until her visits stop. My only regret is that I miss Raymond. He's grown into a man now and no longer plays football. I do miss the hot dogs.

The grocery order I wrote last week is still on the kitchen table and, come to think of it, I haven't seen Neil Fairweather's truck drive past for a few days. I feel a sense of foreboding. Something is wrong.

As I work my way through the few remaining tins of stew in the cupboard of the kitchen dresser, I realise I need to take steps to feed myself. I set traps, but the myxomatosis has all but eradicated the rabbits, and without a gun I cannot bring down a roo or possum.

The logging truck rumbles by, interrupting my thoughts, then feeds a new thought.

I take my axe and select a wattle small enough that I can drag onto the track, but big enough that it will need to be removed for the logging truck to pass. I haul it beside the forestry track, ready to use when the time is right, and return to the kitchen table, retrieving my order. I add some things to it and put the list with a five dollar note into an old envelope I find among Ma's papers stacked on the dresser.

> 6 bananas
> 5 carrots
> packet butter beans
> bottle tomato sauce
> tube of tooth-paste
> cake of soap
> 1 bag potatoes

Next, I scout around for something to use as a flag. A bright orange tea-towel, torn into strips, will serve well.

For the next few days I potter around my hut and vegie garden, collect chook and duck eggs from beneath the tree ferns and wait for the return of the truck as it heads up the mountain.

*

This morning, the logging truck rumbles past, changing down gears preparing for the climb ahead. I recognise the driver and passenger. They are older now, but they are Bob and Arty, two loggers I shared the dugout with ten years before. I feel some comfort in knowing who will carry out my request.

I wait till the sound of the engine fades in the distance then put my plan into action. The wattle trunk lies across the track. Resting on its spreading branches, it stands high enough that the driver will have no option but to stop and pull it from his path. I tie the tea-towel around the middle of the trunk, securing the envelope with my order, then return to my tasks. Waiting.

Late in the afternoon I sit behind the window in my bedroom hut, but as daylight fades, I begin to think my efforts have been in vain. The truck should have returned by now. I leave my post by the window and enter the slab hut to light a fire for my evening meal which, tonight, consists of two boiled eggs and a pot of tea without milk. There is nothing left.

A bright light suddenly sweeps through the darkness. I dash into the front hut and hunker down behind the window just as the truck grinds to a halt. The older of the two men, Arty, climbs down from the passenger door and walks to the tree across his path. He gives it a push with his boot, then turns to call to the driver. I can just make out his voice.

'Give us a hand Bob. It must've blown down in the wind.'

They can't see my note in the dark! I despair.

Bob climbs down and wraps his arm around the base of the tree while Arty grabs the branches at the crown.

'Hang on, what's this?' says Bob. He flicks the tea towel and removes the envelope. He bends to the headlight to read my list and chuckles as he hands it to Arty. I strain to hear what they are saying.

'It looks like a shopping list,' says Arty. Lit by the truck's lights, he turns towards my hut and gives the thumbs up. It seems he knows I am watching. He folds the note and slips it into his shirt pocket, then continues to clear the track.

It will be a few days before I am certain whether my plan has succeeded, but I set to work making a shelter of logs and canvas ready to receive my order.

Three days later, just after daybreak, I hear the truck returning to the mountain. I wait anxiously to see if the driver slows down. If he does, and he delivers my order, my problems are solved for now—later, I will work out what to do in the long term.

Bob walks over to the make-shift shelter, lifts the canvas flap and places a box on the wooden platform. He gives the window a wave as he climbs up into his cab and drives off. When I am sure I am alone again, I retrieve my precious groceries. On top is a bar of chocolate I had not ordered.

I unpack my order and put the vegies in the safe, away from the bush rats. I line the tins up along the shelf on the dresser. At the bottom of the box is a catalogue. I rip open the wrapping of the chocolate bar and as I raise it to my lips, the unmistakable smell of peppermint fills my nostrils. It smells exactly like my toothpaste. I nibble the corner and smile as I thumb through the catalogue pages, looking at so many things I have no use for: farm machinery, clothes, shoes. I tear out this page, as I like the look of the canvas sport shoes. I am sure they would be comfortable and much cooler than my gumboots on hot days. A chill creeps up my spine when I come to the bathroom section with its array of mirrors. Then I stop. A page is full of musical instruments: small keyboards that run on batteries; mouth organs in different keys; and at the bottom of the page—a guitar, complete with a vinyl case and a book of easy-to-follow diagrams of chords. I have no idea what chords are, but I know they will make sense when I read the book.

I rip the page out, draw a thick circle around the guitar and stick the page to my wall. For ten years I had walked up the mountain during winter when I knew no-one was there and played the old guitar until it mysteriously disappeared. How nice it would be to have my own instrument to play whenever I wish.

*

When my guitar arrives on Bob's truck, I am too nervous to take it from its case. I lean it in the corner next to the fireplace. It seems right there. Each morning I brush the ash from the soft vinyl and study the instruction book. What I had hoped would make easy reading is bewildering. There are songs, some I know, and above the words, in little boxes, are lines, circles, numbers, dots but I cannot make sense of them. I sing the words with bitter disappointment, then I notice something: there are the same number of lines above the words as there are strings on a guitar.

I remove the guitar from its case and it glows orange in the firelight. It smells like fresh paint. I strum across the strings and it makes an awful dull noise. Remembering seeing a diagram in the beginning of the book, I find it again and read how each string should be tuned in relation to the one beside it. I turn the silver knob for the thickest string and slowly it tightens until it rings a pleasant sound. Following the instructions, I work my way across all six strings. It makes music far sweeter than the old guitar with rusty strings in the forestry hut. I choose one song, *Red River Valley*, and place my fingers where the circle in the little box indicates. I move on to the next box, and begin to sing along to my very tentative strumming.

Each day I play my guitar until my fingertips burn, but I play on and eventually they become numb and the skin thickens, like the callouses on my hands from chopping wood. I did not think my heart would sing again as it had done when I could draw.

The case has two straps and I put them across my shoulders as a backpack and take my guitar to my cave on Dingo Ridge. The music bounces off the sandstone walls and fills my soul again. I stay for days, lost in my new world, imagining Billy sitting beside me, singing along.

1973

My jaw aches, much as it had done years before when the mailman had driven me to Bairnsdale to visit the dentist. I can't understand why it should ache as I brush my teeth morning and night, always aware that I need to take care of my own health. But the more I brush, the more my gum aches and when I rinse my mouth, the water I spit out is pale pink.

When I next write my grocery order, I add 'pain killers for my tooth' and wait for them to arrive. They numb the pain, but I know this isn't a solution; I need to have the tooth removed. It had worked last time. I take my axe onto Dingo Ridge to continue chopping the peppermint gum log into two-foot lengths for the fire.

*

Minister Matthew Tulloch can see no reason to stop his visits to the Strobridge huts just because Ella has died. He has no worries that Lucy, with her bush skills, can fend for herself, he also knows that, since Neil Fairweather has moved on, the loggers are delivering Lucy's orders, however, when Mrs Skelton, the new owner of Swifts Creek store, tells him that Lucy has written a note on her shopping list asking for pain killers for her tooth, he decides to drop by next time he is in Brookville. He knows he won't be welcomed by Lucy, particularly if he arrives alone, so he asks his sister, Janice to accompany him.

They park in Charlotte Spur Track and approach the slab hut, uncertain what reception awaits them, but all is quiet. Obviously Lucy is not at home. Then they hear the ringing of axe on wood on

Dingo Ridge and circle around the top of the ridge to arrive from above, as if they are out walking.

*

As I raise the axe above my head, ready to strike, a voice from further up the hill makes me start. I had not heard anyone approach.

'Hello Lucy.'

I recognise the man above me on the hill as Matthew Tulloch, the minister who regularly visited Ma in between visits from the Brothers. He has not been near the place since Ma took ill. I rest my axe on the log and wait. A woman emerges from behind the man.

'I've brought my sister along, Lucy. This is Janice. She's a nurse.'

The two visitors take a couple of steps closer, unsure whether I will meet them or bolt. I am curious as to why they have come now, and so I do not move, nor make a sound.

'It's been a while since we visited, hasn't it?'

I remain perfectly still, hoping they will disappear.

'Your mother always made us a cuppa when we visited, Lucy. We're thirsty from our walk. Would you like to make one for us?'

Leaving the axe on the log, I turn downhill and walk slowly towards my hut, my mind in a whirl. This gentle minister is one of the few men that I do not fear. During his visits with Ma, I had peeked through the cracks in the wall and watched him sip tea and make polite conversation. His calm presence had always settled Ma and made her less abrasive. For this, I was always thankful. I can see no reason to refuse him a cup of tea, but am in no hurry to reach the hut. I bend to smell the wildflowers on my way, even pick a bunch to place in a vase on the centre of the table as I had seen Ma do from time to time.

The minister and his sister follow at a distance. I leave the door to the hut ajar and pull the kettle over the fire. He pushes the door open and smiles at his sister. They enter the gloom of the old hut and he pulls two chairs to the table to join me when I take up my usual position facing the fire. Janice removes a packet of biscuits from her bag and places them on the table. Chocolate peppermint. Mrs Skelton must have told her they are my favourites. I grab the packet and rip it open, taking some for myself and chew, careful to avoid the side of my jaw that aches; the crunching of biscuits is all the louder for the silence between the three of us.

The kettle boils and I rise to make a pot of tea, cover it with a cosy, and place three cups on three matching saucers. My visitors know not to expect milk. We sip our tea in silence.

The minister finishes his cup, and I pour him a second.

'I understand you have a toothache, Lucy. Would you like to see a dentist?'

I nod my head slightly but in the dim light, he does not seem to notice. Again, he sips in silence and, deciding nothing is to be gained by delaying the visit any further, rises to take his leave.

'Thanks for the cuppa, Lucy, and for making us welcome,' he says. 'We'll call by again to see how you are faring.'

Janice catches his arm. 'Don't be so hasty. Ask her again, and watch her head.'

He repeats his question: 'Would you like to see a dentist?'

I nod my head again.

'I'll make an appointment and come back for you.'

Again I nod. This time, I smile.

*

I am digging in my vegie patch when a car pulls up and I see the shape of a man getting out from the driver's seat. I run to hide behind a tree.

'Aunty Lucy, if you want to hide properly, you'd better find a bigger tree. I can see you poking out each side of it. What about a cuppa?'

I step from behind the tree and shake my head. I have not seen any family since Maude took Ma away and I do not wish to see any of them now, not even Raymond who has married and moved away from the district.

'I've come to see how you're getting on, now that Ma's not here anymore.'

I turn my back on my nephew.

'Well, I'll go and put the kettle on myself then. You can join me if you want.'

Raymond disappears inside. He calls out: 'I hear you like chocolate biscuits, Aunty Lucy. I've got some peppermint ones here'.

When I enter the hut, he has taken two cups and saucers from the sideboard and placed them beside the biscuits. As I take three, I see Raymond smile; Matthew Tulloch has obviously passed on the information.

Despite my feelings for my sister, I can't dislike this young man who looks so like me. There is no doubting the family chin and nose, and the particular way he holds his head. But why has he come now? We sip and munch in silence for a while.

'Matthew tells me you need to go to the dentist. You know I can take you, if you like. Or shopping. You just need to let me know.'

I reach out for my pad and pencil and write:

no thanks.

I am content with my new arrangements with the loggers and I have already accepted Matthew Tulloch's offer to visit the dentist.

*

A couple of days later, my tooth too sore for me to do anything but sit by the fire, I hear a knock on my door.

'Lucy? Are you there, Lucy?' It's Janice.

I pull the door open a few inches and return to my chair.

Matthew walks in after his sister. 'I have made an appointment with the dentist in Bairnsdale. I believe you have seen him before?'

I nod, knowing that trusting this man is the best way of easing the pain in my mouth.

'I have the car outside and we can go now, if you like. They are expecting us this afternoon.'

I leave the fire and disappear into my sleeping hut. I comb my hair and twist it into a bun on the top of my head, then sit on the side of my bed to change my footwear from rubber boots to sport shoes which are as comfortable as I'd hoped they would be. The mattress sags as I bend to tie the laces.

Matthew and Janice are waiting by their car as I stride from my hut, open the rear door to their car and climb in across to the far side. As I wind down the window, it occurs to me that, if I am going to town, I just might be able to buy a mattress. I fling open the car door and run back to my hut, hearing Matthew mutter: 'Well, it looks like we lost that round,' as I fly past.

'I don't know,' says Janice, 'let's give her a few more minutes, just in case'.

Inside the hut, I remove the bottom drawer from the cupboard beside my bed and, on my knees, reach into the recess and withdraw a brown paper bag filled with notes and coins—the change that comes with my weekly orders. I write a note and stuff it, together with the money, into the deep pockets of my father's old greatcoat, then pull it over my cotton dress.

I walk to the car. Matthew and Janice, sitting in the front seat with the engine ticking over, wait as I climb in again. Janice reaches to lock my door. We set off towards Bairnsdale, an hour later than planned. I wind down both windows. I do not like being confined in the back seat of a car.

Matthew and Janice make themselves comfortable in the waiting room as I walk into the dentist's room. He spends a long time examining my gums and teeth before saying: 'I can't see anything wrong with your teeth, Miss Strobridge. They are in perfect shape. However, you are obviously a bit too conscientious with your cleaning. You have scrubbed so hard, your poor gums are suffering. I suggest you ease up on that, and the pain will go away.'

He steps away, expecting me to rise, but I grip the arms of the chair, dig my heels in and sit firm.

'You can go now, Miss Strobridge.'

I open my mouth and grab the offending tooth with thumb and forefinger and twist, indicating that I want it removed.

'But there is nothing wrong with your tooth.'

Again, I grab it. The dentist looks at the determination in my eyes, and beckons to his assistant.

'If it makes her happy, we'll have to extract it. I can't say I'm easy with this though.'

With my troublesome tooth now gone, I emerge from the room and place my bag of money on the receptionist's counter.

'I think Miss Strobridge means for you to take the payment from it,' explains Matthew. I am pleased he is here to speak for me. The receptionist takes what is owed and hands the bag to me. I stuff it into my pocket and head for the car. Matthew is about to drive off when I thrust a piece of paper into his hand. It contains one word:

mattress

He twists in his seat to face me. 'Do you want to buy a mattress?'

I nod.

'Okay then, we'll go to Myers and get you one.'

In the department store, I charge ahead of my two companions, looking right and left, searching for beds, trying to ignore the people and hubbub. In the far corner I see a flickering screen and deviate from my path to investigate a moving picture playing on the little screen. I pull a chair out from a dining suite on display and watch it with great joy and curiosity. Matthew and Janice stand patiently, waiting for me to resume my hunt for a bed, but I show no intention of moving.

'Have you never seen a television before, Lucy?' asks Matthew.

'Of course she hasn't,' says Janice. 'I bet she's never even been to the movies. It must seem very strange to her.'

From the corner of my eye, I see an attendant sauntering towards me looking distinctly uncomfortable.

'Can I be of any assistance, Sir?' he asks Matthew.

'No, thank you all the same, We are actually looking for a mattress but our friend seems to be taken with your television.'

The attendant points further along the way we had been heading. I sense he would rather I moved on.

'You'll find the bedding department over there, Sir.'

But I do not shift my eyes from the screen. Only when the show finishes do I push the chair back in place by the table and continue on my journey to find my mattress.

I walk up to a bed on display and sit on its edge, bouncing, to make sure it doesn't sag. I bend to untie my laces and remove my shoes, placing them side by side under the bed and lie down. The mattress feels firm, but cradles my body. I fold my hands over my chest and close my eyes, envisaging it in my hut. When I almost drift off to sleep I make the decision that this mattress will do just fine. I sit up and retrieve my sandshoes, bounce on the edge again, just to make sure, then stand and fetch the bag of money from my pocket and empty its contents onto the mattress.

The shop assistant, all this time standing beside Matthew and Janice, looks puzzled.

'I think Miss Strobridge wants to buy the mattress,' says Matthew. 'Just take what she owes from the money.'

'Very strange,' mutters the young man as he selects sixty dollars from the large collection of crumpled notes and walks to the cash register.

Driving home late in the afternoon, with very cold air pouring across my throbbing gums, I smile to myself at the thought of the brand new mattress strapped to the roof of the minister's car.

1976

Sheep Station Creek is dry for the first time in my life. The last time I filled my kettle from the race, there had been more mud than water, and I filtered it through my handkerchief in order to get clear enough water for a cup of tea. I place buckets beneath the overhang of my roof, but they remain empty. There simply is no rain.

I walk for miles along Dingo Ridge track looking for puddles. When I find some water, I light a fire and boil the billy there and then. I have begun adding soft drinks to my weekly shopping list. I find that tea made with lemonade does not need sugar.

*

In his home in Swifts Creek, Matthew Tulloch fills his kettle from the kitchen tap, noticing that the flow slows progressively as the drought increases, and it suddenly occurs to him that Lucy will also be without water. The following Saturday, as the locals gather outside the store to discuss life and the drought, he mentions his concerns.

'I have noticed that Lucy is ordering a large number of soft drinks. Do you suppose that's all she's drinking?' asks Les Skelton.

'Highly likely,' replies Matthew.

Ian Fairweather, the 20-year-old son of Neil, thinks he has the answer. 'There's an old tank at Cassilis that'd do, I reckon. It's not very big, but if we can load it onto the ute, I can bring it down to Lucy's. We'll need to build a stand for it too. Do you reckon she'll let us near the place?'

'Let me approach her first,' says Matthew. 'She seems to be more accepting if I go out there with Janice. I'll let you know how we get on.'

'Well, we'd better make it sooner rather than later,' says Les. 'Poor old dear has nothing to drink, let alone wash in.'

'How will we get water into it, though?' asks Matthew.

'I'm sure the firies will bring a tanker down and fill it,' replies Ian, who has just joined the rural fire brigade.

*

I have noticed that the minister and his sister always wait until I'm on Dingo Ridge, chopping firewood, to visit—or maybe it's that I am so often up here that their visits are bound to coincide with my daily chores. As usual, they appear from further uphill, pretending they are out walking, and call to me; as usual, I ignore them to start with. I don't mind them, they are good people who are only trying to help me, but I don't encourage them as I don't need their help. I don't need anybody's help. I have lived all these years by my own wits and I can see no need to change things now.

'Good morning, Lucy, would you like a cuppa?' He produces a large bottle from behind his back. 'We thought you might like some water.'

I know he knows I have been boiling up soft drinks. He probably also knows that I have been ordering more than the usual talcum powder of late. It appears there are no secrets down at Sandy's store. I leave my axe beside the half-cut log and head downhill, following the track. They follow. He places the bottle in the middle of the table and I carefully measure three cups of water into the kettle. I already have in mind that I will use the rest of the water to sponge myself when they leave. We sit around the table in our customary silence, encircling a packet of peppermint chocolate biscuits.

'Your creek's dry, Lucy. How are you getting on for water?'

I shrug and tip my head towards a pile of empty lemonade bottles in the corner of the hut.

'Surely that's not all you drink?'

'Would you like a water tank?' asks Janice.

I think of having water whenever I want and am about to nod in agreement when a second thought intervenes: in order to have a tank, people—most likely men—will trample all around my home, making noise, scaring the birds and wallabies, talking … I shake my head vigorously.

As if reading my thoughts, Janice adds: 'Maybe we could bring it while you are away, Lucy. Maybe one day while you are in the forest, cutting wood.'

I rise and stoke the fire; this is a decision I cannot make. I walk out and climb Dingo Ridge again. I will camp out in my cave and what will be will be.

*

Matthew and Janice approach Lucy's slab hut, looking for signs that she is there. They knock and wait, but not a sound disturbs the air.

They circle the hut and knock on the door to her bedroom hut. Again, there is only silence.

'You wait here,' Matthew says to Janice, 'and I'll check up the hill'.

He calls to Lucy, but the only sound is his footsteps on brittle dried leaves. He returns to Janice.

'The coast is clear.'

He walks down the forestry track to where Ian's ute, complete with the water tank, is waiting. Behind the ute is Les's truck, stacked with old timber from the mill to make a stand. They roll in beside the two huts, more than a little anxious in case Lucy should appear, wielding her waddy, screaming. They each take a shovel and level the earth between the front door and the corner of her sleeping hut where there will be easy access for the fire truck.

By lunchtime they have levelled a pad and laid the hardwood boards across two solid logs and fixed a length of guttering to the edge of the roof, then they roll the tank—not too big, but enough to hold sufficient water to see Lucy through the drought—from the back of the ute onto its platform.

Early afternoon, a fire truck arrives with a load of water. The firie reverses into position, as close as he can, and secures the fire hose to the outlet. The little group of people cheer as the tank overflows.

Matthew collects Lucy's kettle from the kitchen and fills it from the tap at the bottom of the tank. He places it on the fire, ready for her cuppa.

*

I hear lots of noise coming from my huts: hammering, laughter, the clang of metal. Curiosity gets the better of me and I leave my cave to sit on a rock that overlooks my home. No-one can see me from here, but I can watch the world.

They work far below, like ants scurrying here and there. I know the rains will come again and I will have no use for this contraption they insist on fixing to my home, but perhaps I might use it until then.

I wait until the last vehicle has left before coming down the hill. Steam is rising from the spout of my kettle as I enter, but there is something I need more than a cup of tea. I take down my washtub from its hook near the fire and pour boiling water into it, cooled a little with some fresh water from the tank. Hot water has never felt so good on my body as I wash away weeks of sweat. Then I sit at the table and make a pot of tea.

A week later I hear a familiar knock on the door. Matthew and Janice have come to see how my new water supply is going. I show them by taking the kettle out to the tank and filling it, which makes them smile. As I place three cups and saucers on the table beside the biscuits Janice has pulled from her coat pocket, Matthew says: 'There's something we need to tell you Lucy. My term at Swifts Creek has come to an end. I am very sorry to be leaving all of my parishioners, especially you, Lucy, but you will be in good hands with Father Johnstone. Would you like to put out another cup? He's waiting outside to meet you'.

No, I certainly would not!

I walk to the door and shut it firmly, propping a chair beneath the knob to make sure this unknown 'Father' does not enter. I sit in my chair and pour the tea. I think I am sad that Matthew is leaving the district and I shake the hands he and Janice offer when they leave.

*

Predictably, the drought passes and the rains return as Sheep Station Creek flows once again. I collect my water from the race that is so much clearer than the muddy water rinsing months of accumulated dust from my roof into the tank. I wish I still had a cow to give milk to add to my cup of tea, but Pansy died long ago and I do not know how to buy another cow, so I buy powdered milk from the store. It is nice and rich if I make it double strength.

Years roll on, each the same as the one before. I feel my joints begin to stiffen and find climbing Dingo Ridge a little harder each year, but I am determined not to be a slave to my aging body. When I need a change, I pack some food into an old canvas rucksack and walk over Mount Delusion, building wattle lean-tos to sleep in at night. Sometimes I continue on to the waterfall, but the climb down to the diamond-sparling ferns at the foot of the falls grows a little steeper each time I try. The day will come, soon, when I won't be able to clamber down, and I will feel very sad to say goodbye to this magical place.

As I wander over Mount Delusion, I notice that the undergrowth is not as thick as it used to be when the big fires came through. I have no doubt that this is due to the work of men like Bob and Arty, who continue to deliver my groceries. I have grown used to the sound of the trucks and, while I do not approve of their logging, I have decided that they are not making any permanent change to the forest—no more than I do with my ringbarking—so I no longer bristle at the sound of the chainsaws that have taken the place of their axes.

People try to visit; curious bushwalkers come close when they see smoke drifting from my chimney and knock on my door, or call out 'Hello, is anyone there?' I practise my low guttural growl that scares them away. I see no sense in making cups of tea for people who only want to pry, except, of course, for Raymond. I do not want to meet his wife and family, they mean nothing to me, but I do welcome his occasional visits.

Swifts Creek store changes ownership more than once, but each new owner seems to know of my favourites, including peppermint chocolate biscuits, so this makes no difference to me.

1987

*L*yn Darby is slim and attractive with short dark curly hair and eyes that sparkle like her personality. She and her husband 'Darby' are the new owners of Swifts Creek Store. She has been finding her way around the orders and stock for a couple of weeks when Bob pulls his truck up out the front of the store. It is a favourite part of her work, looking after the needs of those who live in outlying areas and can seldom make the trip to her store. It gives her a privileged look into their private lives, and she is good at keeping confidences. He hands her a brown paper bag.

'Bet you've never had an order quite like this,' he grins.

She removes a crumpled sheet of paper from the bag and scans the rounded letters written with a strong hand and a blunt pencil. A ten dollar note flutters out.

2 meat pies
1 bottle of pickles
tin baked beans
packet velvet soap
piece of cabbage

'How strange,' says Lyn. She turns the bag over, but there is no name; no address. 'Who does this belong to?'

'An old girl called Lucy Strobridge from out at Brookville. Me and Arty have been collecting her stuff for over ten years. Now Arty's retired, it's just me. We've never spoken to her. She used to tie her order to a tree and haul it across the track so we had to stop, but these days she leaves the order in a box beside the track. We

know when there's one to pick up, because she hangs a red rag off the box to let us know.'

'How does she get money to pay for her groceries?' asks Lyn.

'She gets a pension cheque that comes to the post office once a fortnight. What you have to do is send it out when it arrives, and she signs it. Wayne Smith from the bank cashes it for her. He'd know if it isn't Lucy who signs, as she always does it on the back, when she's supposed to sign it on the front—and her signature is pretty distinctive.'

'Does she live alone?'

'Her mum carked it fifteen years ago. She's got a sister somewhere, but as far as we know it's just Lucy. From the amount of soap and toothpaste she buys, she must be squeaky clean. I'll be back this arvo to pick up her stuff and drop it out.'

He bids farewell to Lyn and rumbles off with his full load of logs to deliver to the sawmill.

Filled with curiosity, Lyn gathers together the unusual order. Instead of a piece of cabbage, she selects the plumpest cabbage she can find; chooses the best meat pies—one chicken, and one beef and veg; a large tin of baked beans. She adds a jar of Ponds face cream to the request for velvet soap. She writes a note which she folds into a new envelope along with the change.

Dear Lucy, I'm Lyn Darby and we have just taken over the store at Swifts Creek. I hope we can meet one day. Lyn

She licks the seal closed and writes 'For Lucy' on the front, assuming it will be very unlikely that the two women will ever meet.

*

My order arrives this afternoon and, instead of the usual change in my brown paper bag, there is an envelope with my name written, in a very stylish hand, on the front. I open the envelope and inside is a note to me by someone called Lyn Darby who obviously is the new owner of the store. I didn't know it was being sold. I toss the letter aside. I don't care who runs the store so long as my orders arrive on time.

I am puzzled as I check through my order. What is this Lyn Darby playing at? Still, I open the jar of face cream and sniff its faint perfume. I scoop a dollop out with two fingers and rub it on my hands. It feels nice. I try some on my face. It feels cold as it slides across my skin, but it also feels silky smooth. I take another scoop and rub it along my forearms, feeling the roughness of my skin through the cream. I close my eyes, imagining that the hand that continues to caress my arm belongs to another; to someone who cares enough to touch me as I have never been touched.

I unwrap a firm cabbage from a layer of tissue paper and become more suspicious of this woman. What is she up to, supplying goods I didn't order? I count out the change and check the docket enclosed with the note, but she has not charged any extra. I puzzle long into the night over why a stranger would show me kindness.

*

With each order that arrives, I find a little something extra. Is she trying to get me to spend more money? Her scheme won't work. Despite my better judgement, I begin to look forward to the surprises, but they are not always welcome. I order '1 tin sardines,

1 bottle fish paste,' only to find she has added a tin of herrings in tomato sauce. A rage I had almost forgotten surfaces when I lift the oval-shaped tin from the grocery box. I HATE herrings. Ma always forced us to eat them and they remind me of life before Billy died. I feel ill just at the thought of eating them again. I hurl the tin at the wall that once was Ma's kitchen and my body shakes.

Then there is the time when the silly woman includes teabags. Making tea in a china teapot and drinking it from a china cup on a china saucer is a ritual that enhances my day. Why would I want to use such a thing as a teabag?

When the day comes for me to order some very personal items of clothing, I am relieved the new store owner is a woman. I write my order, so different from the normal groceries:

1 coat
1 hat
2 vests
2 pairs of panties
2 slips
1 pair of sport shoes

They arrive, wrapped in brown paper, tied with string, and a note:

Dear Lucy, I asked Bob to describe you to me so I could get some idea of sizes. He tells me you are bigger than me, with larger feet. Not much to go on, but I hope I have judged right. I have included three different sizes of sport shoes. Please keep them clean and return the ones that don't fit so I will know better next time. Lyn

The largest size is a good-enough fit, so I pack the other two into their boxes and place them in the bottom drawer of my dressing table. They might be useful somehow.

It turns out Lyn Darby is quite resourceful. No matter what I order—blankets, dressing gowns, socks, sheets—she can get them for me. She even cuts the banner from the top of the *Women's Weekly* and adds the magazine to my box, along with all sorts of catalogues. One has a picture of a keyboard operated by batteries. I circle the image and think about it for a long time. I can now play anything I want on my guitar, and sing along, but the strings are very rusty and my fingers are stiffening as I grow older. Perhaps, if I have a keyboard, I will still be able to play songs. Next order, I tear out the page and scribble below the picture:

one of these please

It arrives, complete with spare batteries, and I find to my delight that it is so easy to play. I forget to climb Dingo Ridge for firewood and play it all day, picking out new songs. My fingers don't hurt like they do when I play the guitar, and it is always in tune.

When the batteries eventually fade, I replace them with the spares and order more from the store. This time, Lyn Darby has another surprise for me: a cassette player and with it, half a dozen cassettes.

> *Dear Lucy, I thought, seeing you obviously enjoy music, you might like to play some songs. I don't know what sort of music you like, so I have included some country and western along with some popular songs and some classical music. I hope you enjoy them. Please let me know what is your favourite, so I can get you some more. Lyn.*

I like them all. I like the sound of a human voice singing out from my huts on the side of Mount Delusion.

1988

Raymond sits at my table with his wife, Pat, looking uncomfortable. After putting the kettle on, he tells me to sit down, he has something to tell me. I refuse to sit until I know what he has to say. He rubs his hands together and looks me in the eye.

'Aunty Lucy, I'm sorry, but mother has died.'

The room spins, I stumble into my chair. I have not seen my sister for many years, but always feel she might drop by sometime. Now I know this will never happen. They have all died on me: Billy, Dad, Ma—and now Maude. I can't keep my eyes focussed and feel as if I will collapse onto the floor. I look at Raymond and Pat and see their eyes are filled with tears.

'Her funeral will be held in Melbourne, seeing that's where she lived,' explains Raymond. 'We really want you to be there. You're the only one left from her time.'

I remember my sister who walked with me to the dairy each day, swinging an empty milk can between us; staggering home with it full, careful not to spill any of the precious milk so we would not make Ma mad. We rode together over the mountains, caring for the cattle. The big sister who was always one step ahead of me in life. Now she has taken the final step. I fight the tears as the weight of suddenly being the eldest in the family presses heavily upon me. I can see no reason to refuse Raymond's request.

They drive me to their home at Ensay where Pat has prepared a bed for me to spend the night in readiness for the service the following day. As I walk in through the front door, I can't resist the urge to look around for Ma, to see if Raymond and Pat are still hiding her here. I place a box containing my best dress and fresh undies on the bed and stare out of the window. I do not like the strangeness of it all. I feel I am losing a grip on my life, which has been so predictable until now. Does this mean I can no longer be sure of anything? I do not like change.

Pat calls us all for dinner and as I enter the families' space I see, in the corner of the room, the same box that I had seen in Myers the day I purchased my new mattress. There is a semicircle of easy chairs facing it, so I sit and wait for the pictures to begin. But the screen stays black. Raymond walks in and sees me staring.

'I'm sorry Aunty Lucy, but we aren't able to get reception here, not yet. We bought the TV set to be ready when it comes.'

I'm not sure what he is talking about. Pat calls us to the dinner table and I sit with my nephew and his family, eager to finish my meal to return to the television, hoping to see something. I keep looking towards Raymond, appealing with my eyes to please turn it on. Eventually, I go to bed, puzzled.

We rise early in the morning and I dress in my grey checked dress with pink roses printed over the checks. I saw it in a catalogue and asked Lyn Darby to get it for me. When it arrived, it was far too pretty for me and I have never worn it. Today, I wear it for my sister, along with my newest pair of sport shoes. I tie a scarf over my head, seeing we will be in a church—not that I have any more time for God than I did when Ma was alive, but I feel the family expects it of me.

The minister drones on. I doubt whether he actually knew Maude, the way he speaks. Not like Matthew Tulloch. He would have delivered a very personal eulogy, given half a chance. We walk from the church into the graveyard close by, and I watch as my sister is lowered into a hole in the ground, much as they lowered Billy fifty years ago. Is this how Ma ended her days? I guess maybe now I have to acknowledge that Ma could well be dead too.

*

I return to Brookville and my life continues without change, despite Maude now lying in her grave. In reality, she stopped being a presence in my life so many years ago I have trouble recalling her face. Let the past die with her.

It comes as a surprise when, one day, Ray's wife, Pat, knocks at my door. I peak out through a narrow gap to see her standing on my doorstep with a man I do not know, and I long ago learnt not to trust such strangers.

'Aunty Lucy? I know you're in there. Could you please open the door, we have a surprise for you.'

I remain perfectly still, not moving an inch in case the creak of a floorboard gives me away.

'Darby has brought a television set for you, Aunty Lucy. It's only a little one, but it runs on batteries so you will be able to watch it. We know you would really like one.'

I am sure it is a ruse to get me to open my door, but I see that the man is holding a box in his arms and it does indeed have the picture of a television set on the side. I begin to perspire. I walk softly to my table, without concealing my footsteps, and write a note that I push through a gap in the door.

Leave it on the doorstep

I see Pat pick it up and read it, then show it to the man. He shakes his head and says something to her.

'We really do need to bring it in, Aunty Lucy. Darby needs to set it up properly and make sure you know how to use it.'

I close the door. I know I will probably regret this, but I do not know Darby, who is obviously the husband of Lyn Darby. I do not know if I can trust him, even though he is with Pat. I am happy with my guitar, keyboard, and musical tapes. They drive off after more futile attempts to make me open my door.

1989

Chips Boucher drives his Landcruiser up the long winding climb through ironbark forests growing right to the edge of the road, following Tambo River. It is nice to be coming home after so many years on the track, shearing from shed to shed. Each river crossing is dry. He has returned to take over the family farm on Charlotte Spur Track.

He calls in to the store at Swifts Creek to reprovision and catch up on the latest gossip in the small town, but there is no real news. As he turns the corner on the last leg of his journey, he sees the two old huts and wonders what has become of the strange women who live there. He no longer feels the fear he felt as a kid when he rode past, more afraid of old Ella than Lucy. What was it that made him feel afraid? He no longer remembers, but the huts do still emit an eerie presence. The walls of the back hut are propped up in an attempt to stop them from tumbling to the earth. Surely no-one could still be living there? He makes a mental note to check up next time he goes to town.

*

Word comes from the Swifts Creek mill that logging is to cease on Mount Delusion, which saddens Bob for many reasons. The ash forests have been the centre of his life for nearly fifty years and he has grown to love them. He looks on the mountain hut he, Arty and the boys built after the '39 fires to be his home. He will no longer drive past Lucy's home to deliver her groceries. He drives down the logging track for the last time. Now in his late 60s, he long ago stopped logging, instead, he drives the trucks for the next generation of young men who eagerly drop woolly butt with chain saws.

As he passes the hut, he sees Lucy's box out ready for him to collect her order. Leaving the engine ticking over he walks up to her door—something he has never done—and knocks on the splintery boards. He hears a shuffling noise from inside, but no-one answers his knock.

'Lucy, if you are in there, I'm Bob, and I want to let you know that I won't be able to keep bringing your groceries any more as I have to leave the area. I'm sorry. It's been nice to have been able to help you out, and I'll do my best to find someone else to take over. I only wish we had met some time. Keep well.'

He pats the door affectionately and leaves a small gift on her doorstep before collecting her box and returning to his truck.

*

Bob's words reach my ears bringing anxiety with them. I move to the window and watch his truck disappear around the bend towards Swifts Creek. I have grown so used to his coming and going that I have lost my resentment of the men who log my forest. He leaves a surprise for me on my doorstep: a bottle of cream sherry. I take it inside and pour some into a tumbler and sip. I like the warmth it gives as it settles into my belly.

The days that follow bring complete silence, which I enjoy and resent all at once. I count the tins of food left and wonder if I will be able to feed myself. I check the dozen rabbit traps lying in the corner by the fireplace. They are very rusty, but still work. If necessary, I can resume setting a line of traps. Raymond drops by occasionally and I let him make a cup of tea because he always brings my favourite biscuits.

*

Bob stands at the counter of the Swifts Creek store waiting for Lyn Darby to finish with her customer before handing her the order in its brown paper bag.

'Here you are Mrs Darby, this is Lucy's order, but I'm afraid I won't be able to deliver it as I'm moving on. Perhaps you might know someone who could drop it out there? I do worry about the old girl, you know.'

Chips is just leaving the store when he hears of Bob's dilemma.

'Ah, no worries there mate, I live just along the track from Lucy, I can take it. In fact, come to think of it, I can take over from you as I'm in and out every few days. I've been wondering how the old girls are going.'

'The mother died years ago and Lucy's been pottering along on her own,' explains Bob. I keep an eye out to make sure she looks okay, but never a peep out of her. I'd really appreciate it if you could take over, Chips. Make sure she's travelling well.'

Chips waits for Lyn to assemble the order—she adds a bottle of lime juice cordial as a treat—and he takes the box for delivery. He knows Lucy's reputation for not having contact with people and is determined to change things. He enjoys a yarn and is sure he can draw her into his stories of years in the shearing sheds.

He pulls up near the intersection of the logging track and Charlotte Spur Track and, box in hand, rounds a huge log in front of the huts. Lucy is sitting on a log not twenty feet away. She has her back to him, staring into the distance, and obviously does not hear him approach until he speaks.

'Hello Lucy, I've seen you over the years, but never introduced myself: I'm Chips Boucher, I live just up the track. I'll be looking after your grocery order from now on, and if there's anything I can do for you, you just let me know when I drop by.'

Lucy jumps in fright and puts her hands over her ears and shuts her eyes. Chips laughs at this childlike reaction.

'You'll have to do better than that to hide from me, I can still see you.'

She freezes.

'I'll just leave your box here then.'

He deposits the order in the little slab shelter with its corrugated iron roof, muttering to himself, 'That was a bloody waste of breath!'

The next week, determined to make contact, he takes the box into the hut and places it on her table and shouts her name, but there is not a sign of Lucy. As he leaves, he can hear her high on Dingo Ridge, chopping firewood.

At home, he retrieves a school slate he used as a child and writes on it:

Would you like me to cut your firewood for you? I have a chainsaw.

He leaves it with her order the next week, along with a piece of chalk so she can write her answer. He drives up the road as if heading to Swifts Creek, but around the corner he turns off his engine and hides among the trees waiting for Lucy to come out and rifle through her order, as she likes to do. From the bottom of the box she lifts out the slate and reads what Chips has written, then rubs out his words with her sleeve and disappears into her hut with the slate.

For the next two weeks there is no slate and no reply. Disappointed and frustrated, Chips writes a note on a piece of paper and leaves it in the box:

Give me back my slate or I will come in and get it.

When he returns, he finds the slate, without the chalk, and written in charcoal, one word:

ᴎo

That, thinks Chips, is the end of that. 'You win, Lucy,' he says as he reverts to the years' long practice of simply collecting her box and leaving her delivery.

One time, her order is supplemented by a small gift for her birthday—Lyn has discovered the date from the Centrelink forms that needed to be filled out; other times there are gifts for Easter, Christmas, and all those special occasions Lucy has never celebrated in her life.

1990

Through the 90s, Lucy lives day to day as she has always lived: roaming the mountain; collecting firewood from Dingo Ridge to feed her hungry fire; playing music; tending her vegie garden and chooks. Nothing changes. She is aware that people are worried about the old woman living by herself in a falling-down hut in the bush on the side of a mountain, but she cannot relate to that old woman. In her mind she is as young and strong as she was as a girl and she will never give up her independence.

But the people of Swifts Creek continue to worry about Lucy. She is one of them and they feel responsible for her welfare. Each Saturday morning at Darby's store Chips and Lyn ask the locals who has seen her during the week and how she is getting on. There are reports of seeing Lucy many kilometres from her hut, dressed in a cotton dress and sneakers. It is obvious from the distances she is travelling that she must still be staying out overnight. At least this means she is in good health.

Lyn continues to send her little treats when she fills out her order, and magazines. No request is too difficult for Lyn to fill, even if it means driving to Bairnsdale's stores to purchase a particular coat or mattress Lucy has circled in a magazine with instructions:

one of these please

*

I know that people mean well, but I do wish Lyn Darby would stop trying to change my life. Why does she think I need new things? I don't. I have everything I need right here in my hut. I have all the company I need in my animals. And the trees. They mean so much more to me than people who try to interfere.

I wonder if I could survive without the box of groceries that arrives every week. I check the old traps, but they are frozen solid with rust and I no longer own a rifle, so I must put up with the inconvenience.

2000

The old tank outside is rusting and won't hold water anymore, so I have gone back to placing buckets around the edge of the roof when it rains. This, together with the water from the race, keeps me going. And the bottles of sherry. There is a pile of empties growing outside, next to the empty cans of Irish stew.

But I am worried about something. I have noticed a small lump in my left breast. It isn't causing me any problems, but I do wonder what it might mean. Life seems to be closing in on me of late, I lack the energy to walk the mountains as I used to do.

*

Sitting on a stump, warming my upturned face in the sun, I hear a car pull up. I know it can't be Chips as he had to return to shearing a few months ago. He told me so through my closed door. His role has been taken over by two women from some department or other. Now, they are true busybodies.

I open one eye and see it is Raymond paying a visit. I close my eye again and enjoy the sun.

'Hello Aunty Lucy. I was passing,' (this is a lie, there is no way he was 'just passing' way out here). 'I'll put the kettle on,' he says, disappearing into the hut. I stir my old bones and follow as there is something I need to communicate to him. I wrote a note last week that I have been keeping for his next visit. I retrieve it from my bedroom hut and join him at the cooking fire. I hand him the slip of paper.

I need to talk to Pat about something. It's medical.

'What's wrong?' he asks.

It is very personal, and I can't talk to a man about it. The lump in my breast is getting bigger and it hurts when I lie on it at night. I shake my head and drink my tea.

'I'll bring Pat around tomorrow if you like.'

I nod.

*

The morning is crisp and clear and I wish with all my heart I could wander off into the bush on Dingo Ridge, but I must wait for Pat. I am relieved to find that she is alone when her car pulls up outside. She hurries to me with such a look of concern on her face. I wave her inside and take out a notepad. This conversation will need more than a slip of paper.

I have a lump in my breast. It hurts.

Pat reads my message and her look of concern deepens.

'Oh no, Aunty Lucy. Ma had that too. In the end, it was what killed her. How long have you had it?'

two years

'And you have waited till now to tell me?'

I know she is annoyed.

I didn't want to bother anyone

Pat stands and paces the floor, waving the notepad.

'You didn't want to bother me! For God's sake, we could have done something about it if you'd let us know right at the beginning. Ignoring it won't make it disappear, you know. We need to get you to hospital as soon as we can.'

> I don't want to go to hospital. I'll be alright. I just need something so it doesn't hurt at night.

'No, I'm sorry Aunty Lucy, but this is out of your hands. In fact, I want you to come with me now. We'll collect Raymond—he needs to know; he is family—and take you there today. Come on.'

There is something about the urgency in her voice that makes me obey. I disappear into my bedroom hut and change my underclothes.

As we leave, I write:

> I don't want to have any operation

Pat nods in understanding.

*

Each time I enter Bairnsdale Hospital I shiver involuntarily. My nostrils, which are accustomed to the earthy mustiness of the bush, are assailed by a strong smell of disinfectant and the nervous sweat from other bodies. It takes all my inner strength to keep walking between Raymond and Pat as they steer me to the nurses' station.

Pat speaks in a whisper to a woman dressed in a crisply starched uniform who beckons to another nurse. They, in turn, whisper and look towards me. The second nurse approaches.

'Please come this way, Miss Strobridge.' She takes my arm, but I shrug her off. What makes her feel she can touch my body without my permission?

Pat sees the problem and speaks for me.

'Aunty Lucy, this nurse would like to check you over, if that is okay. Would you like me to come with you?'

It has come to this. I have no option but to allow this nurse to inspect my breast. My mouth dries and I panic. I shake my head. The nurse goes to speak again but Pat holds up her hand to stop her.

'Please, let me handle this.' Then to me. 'Aunty Lucy, we really need to know how bad your breast cancer is.'

There! Someone has finally said the word. Cancer. I've read about it in the magazines Lyn Darby sends and have feared this was the problem. I sink onto a seat, sweating, in shock. Raymond squats before me, holding my hand.

'Aunty Lucy, please let the nurse check you over. I promise nothing will happen without your say so.'

In a daze, I rise and walk towards the curtained cubicle and sit on the narrow bench. I remove my blouse and bra. The nurse enters, apologises for her cold hands, and pokes and prods both breasts, much to my humiliation. A long time ago I had been proud of my body when I had drawn it in such detail, but Ma had told me I was filthy for touching myself. Does this make the nurse filthy too? When I begin to cry, the nurse mistakes my memories for anxiety.

'Sorry Miss Strobridge. Am I hurting you? Try not to worry, I'll be finished soon.'

She would never understand.

*

We are in the Relative's Room, sitting on padded chairs designed to make us feel comfortable, but we feel anything but comfortable. The nurse has called in a specialist who is telling us what alternatives I have.

'The only option is to perform a mastectomy. I suggest both breasts, as it is more than likely the cancer will spread to the right breast. We will then put you on a course of chemotherapy. I don't think the tumour has metastasised, but time will tell.'

Unable to speak, I use the only defence I have. I scream. Raymond and Pat rush to me and lead me out of the room away from the doctor. For the first time in his life, Raymond puts his arms around me.

'We won't let them operate if you don't want. Let's get you home.'

8 JANUARY 2001

I know my days are numbered and I don't mind if it's my time to go. Music now fills my life much as walking the mountains did when I was younger. I have many different keyboards and my demand for new batteries is constant. Once, my yard was filled with vegie gardens and chook pens; now old batteries pile up in a heap next to empty sherry bottles and tins—and the cooking hut, where I spend so much time, is becoming quite cluttered with my music.

Lyn continues to send me cassette tapes and this is the source of so many new songs for me to sing along as I play my instruments. Each month, I look through the magazines and catalogues searching for ideas. I own a collection of mouth organs, although I don't like them as much as the keyboards or the guitar.

It is a curse of living in the mountains that I must keep a constant supply of firewood to feed my fire, summer and winter. The forest of ringbarked trees is dwindling year by year, but I know there will be enough dead trees to see me through.

I retrieve my axe and barrow from beside the hut and make my way up Dingo Ridge to fetch more firewood. I have used all the logs from the last time I chopped down a tree so now I must tap away at the trunks of those dead trees that still stand and select one for this season. I hope there will be one that isn't too large. My strength isn't what it was.

10 JANUARY 2001

Am I awake or in a dream? It is hard to tell. It seems as if I am in the cave on Dingo Ridge, but I am unsure how I came to be here. I shiver feverishly and become aware of an awful pain in my leg. Slowly, memories return of chopping a tree then returning to my hut. Another tree, then the accident. I sit up, painfully, and even in the dim light at the rear of the cave I can see a bloodied bandage covering my ankle. I must get down from here, back to my hut. But how? I would even tolerate interference from a logger, but they left the mountain years ago. Calling for help is of no use. The only sounds I can make are those of the wild animals, and I have used them for so many years to repel visitors no-one would know that this time their attentions would be welcome.

It takes the best part of the day to inch my way down the slope, sliding on my bottom. Halfway down, I remember I have left my axe and barrow on the ridge. They will have to wait, but I fear they will be ruined if left out in the weather—or worse, stolen.

When I reach level ground around my hut I grab a stout stick and struggle to my feet and hobble to the door. The pile of ashes in the corner, usually glowing pink, has no life, confirming that I have been in the cave for days. I test the weight of the kettle for water—some sloshes inside—and light a bundle of kindling on top of the ash pile. Hopping on my good leg, I go to my sideboard and lift down a shoebox that holds my collection of bandages and medicines. I add a good splash of Dettol to the baked enamel washing-up dish. The room fills with its pervasive smell as the brown liquid turns milky when I add the boiling water.

I ease the blood-encrusted bandage from the wound. Very few things in life bring fear to me, but as I look at the broken end of my bone through a window of ragged flesh, my stomach churns and I gag.

The hot liquid on the cotton ball stings unbearably as I begin to bath my ankle. I can't control my stomach and dry retch as the room spins, then goes black.

12 JANUARY 2001

Strips of bark and spider webs dangle between branches that prop up my drooping roof. They blur and swim before my eyes as I try to focus. I am not sure if the gnawing in my gut is hunger or fear. I right the upturned chair lying beside me and pull myself up against the table. Again, my fire is cold, but the ache in my leg isn't so bad. I reach for the basin and resume bathing with the now-cold wash. Dried blood rims the weeping wound. Healing has commenced. I select a good-sized bandage from the shoebox and wrap my ankle, mainly to keep it clean. My hair is in a tangle I can't comb. Without a second thought, I gather it behind my neck and cut it with the kitchen scissors. I can't remember the last time I have worn my hair so short.

A biscuit would be nice, but the food cupboard doesn't contain anything other than boxes of tea and tubes of toothpaste. I tear a page from the exercise book and write:

> 3 bags butter nut snaps
> 1 mint chocolate
> 1 cadbury chocolate
> Very strong pain killers for my sore leg

I fold it around a twenty dollar note and place it in a brown paper bag in a cardboard box. I will take it out tomorrow. Night falls but I cannot make my way to my bed, so I sit in the chair but don't sleep. A fever takes hold and I hear voices from the past. A cheeky, pointed face smiles at me, stroking my hair from my face.

Billy? Is that you Billy?

Billy's face fades and another takes its place. A stern face framed by a circle of plaits. An angry face.

No! Not you Ma! Give me Billy back.

I wish for a fire, but the heat from my body takes its place. Visions continue to dance before me: I am once again a young girl on my mountainside.

13 JANUARY 2001

Confusion and hunger cloud my mind. The smell from my ankle grows steadily worse and now flies settle on it. I spend all my time waving them away from my wound and notice an increasing red circle. My ankle feels hot to the touch. My fear increases. There are times that I lose consciousness and when I wake, the flies have settled again. I should keep it bandaged, but it is weeping and I would rather continue bathing it. I am beginning to doubt it will heal.

Rain begins to fall and I need water, so I lean heavily on my stick and go outside to reposition a bucket below the dripping roofline. Ironically, I lean on the little tank that rusts into the ground below guttering clogged with leaves. Back inside, I unscrew the lid of a bottle of cream sherry and fill my cup. Perhaps it will dull the pain.

My world shrinks to a battle with flies and the hunt for easy food. I have no sweet biscuits, but my tube of toothpaste tastes much like the peppermint biscuits, so I squeeze some onto a cracker and eat that. My stomach rebels at the mixture and I vomit again.

I find an unopened tin of Spam on the bottom shelf of my food safe. It takes another day to summon the energy to find my tin opener. I am afraid I may be dying.

I feel something wriggle on my ankle and think it is a leech. But leeches aren't white, and there are so many! I stand, sway, then collect my walking stick and walk to the door, steadying myself on the wall with my spare hand.

I think I hear someone calling my name and contemplate calling out in response, then change my mind. I don't want anyone invading my world, especially not now. If I am to die, I want to do it as I have lived my life, without intrusion of bothersome do-gooders.

*

Time loses meaning. Lucy takes an hour to collect a half-bucket of water drained from the roof and return to the fireplace. But there is no warmth to boil the kettle. Confused, she pours cold water onto leaves in the teapot and waits for the tea to draw.

In Swifts Creek, Lyn Darby cannot quell an uneasy feeling that Lucy is in trouble and the worry stays with her throughout the night. For two weeks, she has not received an order in the distinctive handwriting. In years past, this had not been a worry as Lucy would wander over the mountains for days at a time, but these days she remains close to her hut and her orders have been regular as clockwork. In the morning, Lyn rings Chips, who is home for a few weeks between shearing contracts, and explains that Lucy has not left her order out, as usual, and asks him to please take a look.

Chips knows there is no use trying to approach Lucy's hut directly, so he settles down behind a large log beside the track to watch.

The two women from Human Services arrive to collect Lucy's order from her box, unaware that she lies, semi-comatose, within her hut. Unusually, there is no box, but they are only paid to collect her order and deliver her groceries, so they do not feel it is their job to also take care of Lucy. Chips emerges from his hiding place and approaches the women to discuss the problem, but they turn on him, asking what he is doing here. After all he has done over the years, his temper flares.

'Look, I don't care what you think, we have a problem here and we need to get help for Lucy. We really need to find out what's going on.'

'Why? What's it to you,' replies one of the women. 'You should be ashamed of yourself, hanging around, spying on an old woman.'

'I don't need to put up with this shit!' says Chips, and climbs into his truck and heads straight for Bob Williams, the police sergeant.

When they return, the two women have left the scene and still there is no smoke from the chimney; no sign that Lucy is moving around her hut. They squat behind the log again, assessing the situation; although in truth, they are summoning the courage to approach the old woman known for her temper.

The police sergeant calls out: 'Lucy, it's the police here, I've come to see how you are. To see if you need any help'.

He is about to give up and leave when Chips pulls his arm and points towards the door to the old slab hut. It opens a crack, then a little wider. Chips is shocked to see Lucy, stooped over two sticks, stumble from the door then fall to the ground.

'Oh shit,' says the sergeant, 'we've got a problem alright'.

Chips jumps up to race to Lucy, but the sergeant grabs his arm.

'No Chips, we'll only frighten her, we'd better do this properly. I'll fetch the bush nurse and come back.'

With nothing else for him to do, Chips waits behind the bushes, watching, wishing he could spare the old girl the inevitable interference that will follow. Half an hour later he hears the siren of an ambulance followed by two police cars approaching.

'Oh God, the poor dear. This is the worst thing that can happen to her.'

14 JANUARY 2001

Even with my eyes closed, I know I am in Bairnsdale Hospital. It's the sterile smell as much as anything, but also the squeak of soft-soled shoes on smooth shiny floors and the lack of fresh air. The temperature does not change, nor does the light. This is unnatural.

I can no longer feel the pain in my ankle, but I know it is due to morphine and not because it is healing. Perhaps it won't heal. Perhaps it is this that will take me, not the cancer. I have often wondered how I will die and I thought it would be on the mountain among my trees, not in a brick building surrounded by so many ill people. It doesn't seem fair.

A nurse comes to look at my wound and I see her gag. She must be new. She is very young. She rushes off and returns with an older nurse; she calls her 'sister'. They inspect my ankle together then they both disappear and return with a doctor and they huddle and whisper. The doctor comes and perches on the edge of my bed.

'Lucy, may I call you Lucy?' he doesn't wait for my answer, 'I'm sure you're aware that you have a very serious injury to your ankle. It's been over a week now and shows no sign of healing and it will almost certainly turn gangrenous. I think it is best if we amputate your foot to above your ankle. I know this probably comes as a shock, but really, it will save your life in the end. I'll get sister to fetch the paperwork for you to sign'.

I cannot look him in the eye. There is no way I will agree to having my foot amputated. The doctor has absolutely no idea what sort of life I lead and how this is impossible. I will not sign the form.

I'm prepared to die, but not here, not with the memories this hospital holds for me. He pats my leg as he departs. Why do people think they can touch me without asking?

I drift off again and take my mind to my mountain. Mount Delusion. It only now occurs to me what a strange name it is.

When I open my eyes again, Raymond is sitting by my bed, his chin resting on his clenched fist. I have never seen him look so worried.

'Is it sore, Aunty Lucy?'

I shake my head, which makes me feel dizzy.

'They've probably doped you up.'

I nod, but again I feel dizzy, then overwhelmingly nauseous. Raymond reaches for a dish and holds it under my chin as I vomit. I am mortified.

'The doc says he wants to chop your foot off. You don't want that, do you?'

I shake my head vigorously.

'I didn't think so. What do you want?' He pulls a notebook and pencil from his pocket and hands it to me.

> If I have to be in hospital, I want to go to Omeo to die. I want to be buried in the cemetery there, with Ma and Dad.

'I thought you might. Don't worry, I'll make arrangements. They'll probably take you by ambulance. Would you be able to cope with that?'

I shrug. I have no choice in the matter.

*

Chips cannot sleep. He tosses, turns, makes a cuppa and walks outside to cool off. He wonders if he could have done anything to prevent the chaos of the past twenty-four hours. He cannot forget the look of terror on Lucy's face as the bush nurse and the ambulance driver laid her on a stretcher and wheeled it to the rear of the ambulance. He is also worried about her huts. Her possessions. He's sure no-one from the district would enter and steal things, but these days there are more and more people from outside who wander past. Curiosity might just make them investigate. By six o'clock in the morning he can't bear the torment any longer and he rings Raymond.

'Mate, I think we should get over there this morning and make the place secure. What do you reckon?'

'Yes, I think we should, but we might take Bob with us. We don't want people talking about us robbing Aunty Lucy.'

'Smart move. I'll meet you there at eight.'

Chips hasn't been inside the hut since the first day he delivered Lucy's groceries twelve years before. Then, it had been old but everything was in its place, as neat and tidy as Lucy herself. Today, he is confronted by utter chaos. He flicks his torch around the blackened walls, most of which are propped up by crooked branches. Spider webs hang from sheets of fibrous bark that threaten to collapse. Hundreds of boxes of matches are scattered around the fire, itself a pile of ash half a metre high, festooned with dozens of burnt-out kettles. How on earth did she ever cook on this? Axes without handles, handles without heads, brooms by the dozen, their straw worn to stubs. Under a low roof to the side, a mountain of boxes that once had contained grocery orders all have envelopes with receipts from Lyn and the change from each purchase. Rusty rabbit traps.

He walks out the door and into the gap between the two huts. Thirteen hand-made wheelbarrows, some without wheels, some without handles, litter the walkway. In her bedroom, he lifts twenty-five blankets from her bed. The drawers of an old dresser beside the bed have forty-eight new pairs of sneakers, still in boxes, and eight pairs of gumboots. Wherever he shines his torch, there are piles of papers, boxes, bags.

But there is no Lucy.

Chips sits on the doorstep to the bedroom hut, overwhelmed with sadness. Lucy has been here most of his life, but she will not be returning.

*

Omeo Hospital is everything Bairnsdale Hospital isn't. On a rise, it has windows that open to the summer breeze. There are no loud noises, traffic, car horns, sirens. The nurses don't rush. It is almost peaceful. I close my eyes and drift off.

I wake but keep my eyes closed. I can hear someone breathing beside my bed. Then a voice speaks and I recognise it immediately. Chips.

'Gidday Lucy. Do you know who I am? It's Chips, I used to deliver your groceries a few years back.'

I open one eye and have a peak at him. He's smiling, but I can see a worried look around his eyes. I certainly don't want to get into any conversation with him, but I feel I owe him some acknowledgement. I nod my head and close my eye again. He stays seated for a long time, then finally leaves so quietly, I can barely hear his footsteps.

I have another visitor in the afternoon. This time, I don't recognise the voice that greets me. It is a woman.

'Lucy, I'm Lyn Darby. I'd like to introduce myself as the woman who has been sending your orders for the past fifteen years. We've never met, but I feel I know you so well. I'm sorry you are here. Please let me know if there's anything I can do.'

I can't resist the urge to open an eye and see what this Lyn Darby looks like. I am surprised. I expected a dowdy shopkeeper but she is an attractive young thing with dark curly hair. There is no denying she has made a huge difference to my life, buying clothing for me, introducing me to so much music—and chocolate peppermint biscuits. There is too much to say, so I say nothing. Maybe she notices the tears that escape from my tightly closed eyelids.

*

My time is coming soon. I can't move my leg and it is beginning to smell. They no longer try to feed me food but hold a little box of some milky liquid to my lips. I suck through the straw. It tastes awful. I can't always swallow and the nurse holds a tissue to my mouth as I spit it out. It appears I am now totally reliant on other people. This is not how I want to end my days.

Lyn Darby visits again this afternoon. I am propped up against some pillows when she sits on the chair beside my bed. She digs into her handbag and produces my favourite biscuits. My appetite returns and I hold out my hand for them. Before handing them over, she clasps my hand in hers.

'I am so pleased to finally meet you, Lucy.'

This time, it is she who has tears in her eyes. I take the packet and clutch it to my chest and close my eyes.

EPILOGUE

On 13ᵗʰ February 2001, Lucy Strobridge dies in Omeo Hospital. Brookville loses a unique woman, but a legend is born.

The day of her funeral, Chips and his wife return to Lucy's huts and climb Dingo Ridge. Chips plucks a branch of peppermint gum flowers to lay across her coffin. At his insistence, he acts as a pall bearer.

The woman who had lived alone on the side of Mount Delusion, refusing to communicate her whole life, would have been very surprised that so many watched as her white coffin, sparkling with gold, was lowered into an unmarked grave beside her Ma and Dad.

*

When wildfires spread through the district in 2003, they say that Lucy's spirit saved the huts from burning. I would not be at all surprised.

ACKNOWLEDGMENTS

Many have provided information on the life of Lucy, and without them, this story could not have been written. So thanks go to: Chips and Gracie Boucher for trusting me and sharing so many personal stories and photographs; Ray and Pat Carey for giving me insight into their aunty; Lyn Darby who looked after Lucy's orders with dedication; Norm Endacott, Ken Baird and Noel Fraser for timber industry information; Norm Cameron who relayed anecdotes on his visits to see Lucy; Tom and Helen Sandy who lived next to Lucy for many years; Beverley Cook; Peter Crisp; Neil Strobridge; Ian Fairweather; Marion Fraser (nee Fairweather); Victorian High Country Huts Association.

Thanks also to my friends Pam Cole, Warne Wilson, my partner Doug Eaton and my daughter Liane Milligan for reading early drafts and making valuable comments.

And Graham Scully of Kosciuszko Huts Association for taking me to see the Strobridge huts in 2005.

The following books have also proved valuable in gathering information for this story:

Whispers from the Mountains by Laurie T. Boucher

Awakening of a Jehovah's Witness: Escape from the Watchtower Society by Diane Wilson

Lucy Strobridge: Maid of the Mountains by Bob Bates

Forests of Ash: an Environmental History by Tom Griffiths

Victoria's Alpine Heritage: The Huts of the High Plains Bogong, Dargo & Hotham Regions by Fiona Magnussen

Cover images:

Mighty Mountain Ash and Tree Ferns – Shutterstock, Norman Allchin

Lucy's Hut in Snow – Chips Boucher

Dale Lorna Jacobsen

Dale Lorna Jacobsen is a freelance writer who has the good fortune to live in the bush just outside Maleny, Australia. She is passionate about grass-roots history, which led to the publication of two novels: *Union Jack* (2011), political intrigue set in Queensland in the 1920s; and *Yenohan's Legacy* (2013), a story of love and life in the High Country of Australia. In 2013 she fulfilled a life-long dream, taking part in an expedition to Antarctica, and produced an ebook, *Why Antarctica? a Ross Sea odyssey* in 2015.

Contact details:
email: dalelornajacobsen@bigpond.com
facebook: www.facebook.com/dalelornajacobsenauthor
postal: PO Box 456, Maleny, Queensland, Australia 4552